PRAISE FOR *SCRITCH SCRATCH*

"A teeth-chattering, eyes-bulging, shuddering-and-shaking, chills-at-the-back-of-your-neck ghost story. I loved it!"

—R. L. Stine, author of the Goosebumps series

"A spine-tingling blend of hauntings and history."

—*Publishers Weekly*

"Mary Downing Hahn fans will enjoy this just-right blend of history and spooky."

—*Kirkus Reviews*

"[A] scary tale that lives up to the reputation of haunted Chicago... Offers a ghost-hunterly blend of reality and chills that should appeal to many readers with creepy interests."

—*The Bulletin of the Center for Children's Books*

PRAISE FOR *WHAT LIVES IN THE WOODS*

"Currie...throws all the frightfully fun trappings of haunted-house tales at readers, who will soak up the stormy nights, town rumors, exploding light bulbs, creeping shadows, unsettling whispers... Light horror for larger collections."

—*Booklist*

"A perfect middle grade horror selection...holds its own as a shivery stand alone."

—*The Bulletin of the Center for Children's Books*

"The scares are real, the resolution satisfying, and a sequel would be welcome... A thrilling read with an engaging protagonist."

—*Kirkus Reviews*

"An appropriately tween horror story in staccato chapters with plenty of goose bumps."

—*School Library Journal*

PRAISE FOR *THE GIRL IN WHITE*

"Charming and chilling in equal measure, I absolutely fell in love with Mallory and with the mist and the ghosts of Eastport."

—Katherine Arden, *New York Times* bestselling author of the Winternight trilogy and the Small Spaces quartet

"Currie's middle grade novel brims with tension, spine-tingling terror, and convincing characters bravely facing a supernatural dilemma."

—*Publishers Weekly*

"In tense, fast-paced chapters, Currie concocts a chilling setting replete with haunting spectral scares...chillingly rendered."

—*Kirkus Reviews*

"A satisfying spooky selection... Would recommend this to kids... looking for a Goosebumps-style read."

—*Youth Services Book Review*

ALSO BY LINDSAY CURRIE

The MYSTERY of LOCKED ROOMS

To Ella. You are kind, caring, and strong. We may not know

which campus you'll land on next year, but we know that

college will be lucky to have you. Fortune favors the bold.

Published by Sourcebooks Young Readers, an imprint of Sourcebooks
P.O. Box 4410, Naperville, Illinois 60567–4410
(630) 961-3900
sourcebooks.com

Cataloging-in-Publication Data is on file with the Library of Congress.

This product conforms to all applicable CPSC and CPSIA standards.

Source of Production: Lake Book Manufacturing, Melrose Park, Illinois, USA
Date of Production: December 2023
Run Number: 5033193

Printed and bound in the United States of America.
LB 10 9 8 7 6 5 4 3 2 1

The

MYSTERY

of

LOCKED

ROOMS

LINDSAY CURRIE

sourcebooks
young readers

CHAPTER ONE

LASERS AND LAVA

"Angle it the other way!" West screeches, holding his mirror up in the air. Sweat beads on his forehead, and his eyes are wild with excitement. We're going to beat the clock this time. We have to. "Toward the door!"

Lasers are a pretty common thing in escape rooms. I've heard it's because there's a famous scene in a movie about someone named *Indiana Jones* where the hero uses a laser beam to light up an important room. I haven't seen the movie yet, but I get it. Lasers are fun. Sometimes in escape rooms, you have to avoid crossing them or an alarm goes off. Other times, like now, you have to figure out how to get a specific laser beam to land on an object in the room—like a target. Once you do, the beam usually unlocks a door or a clue. If you have mirrors and you understand angles, it's totally doable...but hard.

I tilt my mirror slightly, stopping when the red beam of light begins to travel across the wall. My goal is to reflect it from my mirror to West's, but getting the angles right is tricky. We've already tried twice. Hopefully the third time is the charm.

When I finally get the light onto West's mirror, I exhale in relief and focus on keeping my hands steady. "Okay, you need to tilt yours just a little bit now, West. Not too much. Like ten degrees or so. And Hannah... Don't. Move."

Hannah's eyes flick toward me, then immediately back to West. She looks like a frightened mannequin, all stiff and uncomfortable as she struggles to keeps her mirror at the exact angle we think it needs to be at to reflect the beam.

"Okay, here we go. Everyone pray. Or...whatever you do." As he begins tilting his mirror, West's tongue shoots out of his mouth. He always looks like this when he's focusing. Like a frog about to catch a fly.

The beam glides from West's mirror across the far wall, eventually making its way to Hannah's mirror. It moves onto the glass and then bounces off, reflecting back across the room and onto a small button above the door.

A familiar sound echoes through the room. The

click-thunk of a door unlocking. And then, the high-pitched wail of the buzzer.

We did it!

Letting out a loud whoop, I lower my arms and wince. My muscles are burning. My hands are shaking. My brain is fried. But still, I'm the happiest I've been in a loooooong time. *Lasers and Lava* is the second-hardest escape room at Escape City, and we just beat the buzzer.

West collapses on the floor like he just won Wimbledon. "I can't believe we did that!"

Hannah rushes over and throws her long arms around me. Blond hair flies into my face.

"Aaaeeeeeeeeeeyeeee! Only the seventh team in the entire *Lasers and Lava* history to beat the clock, amirite?" She pulls back and gathers her hair, tying it up in a sloppy bun. Thank goodness. One more flick and I might lose a cornea. "But if anyone was going to do it, it was us. Long live *the Deltas!*"

I grin at her use of our nickname. We came up with it last year, in sixth grade, because Hannah, West, and I are pretty much inseparable. Plus, we all love math and numbers. Like three sides of the same triangle, none of us can imagine what life would be like if we weren't together. Without any one of our sides, our triangle would be nothing but a big ol' *L,* and everyone knows *L*s are for losers.

"We get a T-shirt this time, right?" West asks, dragging himself off the floor. "The last prize was a laptop sticker. But this was seriously hard."

It *was* hard. Thank goodness Hannah has such good balance, because some of the hidden objects we needed to find were in a room where you had to pretend the floor was made of lava. You couldn't just walk across it; you had to use a black light to see a pattern in the tiles on the floor, then hop through the room on just those tiles. If you fell off the safe tiles and touched a different part of the floor, it added five whole seconds to your timer. Five seconds! Thanks to Hannah's history in ballet, she didn't fall off even once. She snagged all the hidden objects, got across the room in record time, and pushed a button that allowed West and I to run across normally.

West had his job cut out for him too. He's always been good at riddles, but the ciphers in *Lasers and Lava* were super hard. It helps that he has the best memory of anyone I know. The guy can remember the most random stuff.

I was our decision-maker. Ever since starting to learn about probabilities, I've loved them. If you understand probabilities, you understand risk. And taking too many risks in an escape room is a bad idea. I was the one who figured out we could afford to ask for exactly one hint during this game and still not add too much time onto our total.

"Um, not just a T-shirt. We get our names on"—Hannah pauses, then makes a drumroll sound with her mouth—"the big board!"

The big board. Ho-ly cow. We've been on it before, of course, but not for escaping a room this hard. Over three hundred groups have attempted this room, and only six of them finished it in less than an hour.

But the Deltas did. I do a little fist pump before gathering my phone from the bucket we were asked to put them in when we arrived. Honestly, I don't know why they even take cell phones away. Even if you were dumb enough to pay good money to go to an escape room and cheat, there wouldn't be time—not enough to look up all the riddles and codes and get the answers, anyway.

We make our way into the lobby, each of us still vibrating with adrenaline. The T-shirts are blindingly yellow, but I don't care. It's all about the memory for me. The achievement. The feeling I get when we escape a room isn't too different from when I do really well on a math test. I might not be as bold as Hannah or as funny as West, but at least I know my numbers. Unlike other subjects in school, math feels simple to me. There is only one right answer. Same with escape rooms. If you take your time and follow the pattern, you'll get out.

I make a mental note to say thank you to Aunt Jeannie

for this. She sent me a membership to Escape City as an early birthday gift. Without that, I probably wouldn't have been able to come here today.

"Smile, guys!" Hannah chirps, angling her cell phone out so she can take a selfie with West and me. We look wild, flushed cheeks, mussed hair, and our neon T-shirts, but still, I'm warm inside. Happy.

If I didn't have to go home, this day would be perfect.

CHAPTER TWO
MOM NEVER CRIES

There's a yellow paper stuck to our door, waving in the breeze when I get home. Probably a notice that we missed a delivery or something. Not that anyone in our house is doing much online shopping these days, but whatever. Still sticky with sweat from the escape room, I quickly tug it free and head inside.

"Mom?" I call out, knowing full well she's still at work. There are twenty-four hours in a day, and right now, it feels like Mom works for twenty-three of them.

I set the paper down on Mom's desk, sighing at the heaps of clutter. I'm not a neat freak, but this is messy, even for me. A half-eaten plain bagel teeters on the edge of the desk, surrounded by partially opened envelopes. I scan a few, frowning when I realize what they are. Bills. Dozens and dozens of bills.

Letting my eyes flutter closed, I replay the end of the escape room in my mind. The adrenaline rush of hearing that last door click open was *awesome*. I mean, we defeated a room that only six other teams have escaped. Six! *Lasers and Lava* is the second-hardest room at Escape City, and my brain helped us beat it.

Too bad I never feel half that useful here at home.

I'm about ready to throw a mini pizza in the microwave when Mom bursts through the front door.

"Oof, Sarah, can you give me a hand?" She's in a pair of worn blue scrubs—the ones she has to wear when she goes to work as an assistant at the local dentist's office—and juggling a strange assortment of bags and...fishbowls? "Vanessa needed me to pick up some new storage containers for the shop, but I seem to have run out of hands!"

I take two of the bowls out of her arms and set them on the kitchen counter, laughing. Leave it to my mom to buy fishbowls to use as candy jars. Then again, she's probably the only person on earth to work at a dentist's office *and* a candy store. Maybe it's a good thing. The more candy she sells, the more patients her boss, Dr. Rose, will have.

Shrugging out of her jacket, Mom eyes the frozen pizza

on the counter. "Oh no, you don't. I hardly ever cook for you kids anymore. Tonight, I'm going to!" With this she begins pulling things out of the plastic bag. Broccoli, potatoes, and... chicken. Actual chicken too, not the plant-based kind.

I smile, even though my heart is crumpling. I'm a vegetarian and have been for a year, but it's one of those things I don't expect Mom to remember anymore. She's already stretched so thin as it is. Plus, it's not like I do much to help around here. I'm too young to get a job or make a dent in the bills. The least I can do is pretend to eat meat, even if that means going to bed with a growling stomach.

"Have you been up to check on your father?" she asks as she begins unwrapping the chicken.

I shake my head. "Just got home, but I can."

"Thanks, honey. I only have an hour before I have to be at the shop, so I want to get this dinner going. Can I rely on you and Seanie to take it up to your father later?" she asks, jumping backward as water sloshes out of the pot she's carrying and onto her scrubs.

"Of course," I say, snorting at her use of my older brother's nickname. Sean is eighteen, six foot three, and applying to colleges, but Mom still calls him Seanie, which makes him sound like a toddler. "Be right back."

My legs feel like lead as I climb the steps up to Dad's

room. Two years ago, he was the most energetic person on earth. Mom joked that he was aging backward and that if he kept going at that rate, she'd need to find the fountain of youth to keep up with him.

Then everything changed. Dad suddenly slowed down. Like, *way* down. He said it felt like trying to recover from the flu, only he never had the flu. The first six months were terrible, like someone turned off a light switch in him. He slept most of the day, and when he was awake, he was moody and sad. The next six months weren't much better. And when the doctors finally diagnosed him, that's when our awful new reality set in. No one knows what causes chronic fatigue syndrome, CFS for short, or how to get rid of it. So pretty much he's just going to be tired the rest of his life, and there's nothing any of us can do about it.

Dad's room is dark, save for some slivers of light coming through his window. I crack the door open just long enough to hear the deep inhales and exhales that tell me he's asleep. Narrowing my eyes on his nightstand, I can see there is still water in the pitcher we keep next to it. His red button is still within arm's reach too. We almost got him a bell when the stairs became too hard for him, but Sean thought the big red button was better. Every time Dad pushes it, it makes an applause sound. It was cute at first, but now every time I hear that clapping, my stomach churns.

There's nothing good or applause-worthy about my dad being stuck in bed. Nothing.

I gently close his door and creep back downstairs. Mom isn't in the kitchen anymore. She's by her desk, the yellow paper I found stuck to the front door fluttering from her hand down to the floor.

"Mom?" I ask, worry prickling me. "Is everything okay?"

She takes a deep breath and releases it with a small shudder. Swiping at her eyes with the back of her sleeve, she stays silent. Still, I can see her shoulders shaking.

Mom is crying, and Mom never cries.

Crossing the room, I reach down and pick up the paper. Written in bold letters across the top are three words...words I'll never forget seeing for the rest of my life.

NOTICE OF FORECLOSURE

CHAPTER THREE
THE TRIPLET TREASURE

It turns out foreclosure is a terrible thing, and Mom knew about it for a long time. Since she can't afford to make the payments on our house, the bank wants to take it back.

Who takes back a whole house? It's not like a borrowed pencil or something. It's our home!

Hannah snakes an arm around me as I use my sleeve to soak up another round of tears. I knew things were bad, but I didn't think they were *lose our house* bad.

"I'm so sorry," she whispers. "I don't even know what to say."

"Me either," I sniff out. "I just can't believe it."

West is sitting in the corner of his room, staring off into space. He's hardly said anything since I called an emergency meeting of the Deltas and dropped the bomb on them. I'm not surprised. As outgoing as he can be, West also worries a lot. He says it's usually at night when everything is quiet and his room is dark, but I know there are other times too. Now seems like one of those times.

"There has to be a solution," West says, finally looking at me. His green eyes are crinkled with concern. "This is fixable, right? Everything is fixable." He says this last part like he's trying to convince himself.

I shake my head grimly. "I don't think it is. Not without a lot of money, anyway."

"How much does your mom owe?" Hannah asks. There's a note of hesitation in her voice, probably because people usually feel awkward talking about money. I don't though. Hard to feel awkward about something you don't have.

"She didn't say, but it must be bad."

Just thinking about Mom working as hard as she does and keeping a secret like this makes me sad. She's always smiling, always reminding us to be grateful for what we have. Unfortunately, what we have is about to get a lot smaller. It's so unfair.

"We need a winning lottery ticket," Hannah mumbles. "Or maybe we could get on a game show. Oooh, even better, we could find that funhouse treasure!"

"Pffft," West says. "The Triplet Treasure? No way. There's nothing hidden in that place. If there were, someone would have found it by now."

Aaaand I'm officially lost. "Triplet Treasure? What is that?"

West lets out a loud snort. "Seriously, Sarah? You haven't heard those stories? The funhouse is only like fifteen miles from here!"

"I did just move here three years ago. Cut me some slack." I frown. Not at the moving in part; that was great. For the first time in my life, I felt like I belonged. I was the person West and Hannah were missing too, the third side of the triangle.

We met the summer I moved to Park Glen. West and Hannah were in her front yard trying to figure out how to get her cat out of their giant oak tree. Instead of just climbing up, they were creating a ramp out of bits and pieces of things. An old plank of wood was their base. From there, taped-together cardboard ran up to the side of the tree, where it was attached to the trunk. Under the cardboard, they created two braces with a set of crutches. One was adjusted longer than the other to keep the taller part of the ramp from collapsing. A thin line of cat food trailed down the cardboard ramp. I guess they thought it would lure the cat down. The whole thing looked sketchy and dangerous, even for a cat.

I probably shouldn't have, but I stopped and watched. It was funny how these two kids I didn't know were plotting to save a cat that, based on the way it was growling, did not want to be saved. It was also funny because even then I could tell their odds of getting the cat to jump down and onto that ramp were not good. When they caught me staring, I told them that, and then they did the most unexpected thing. They asked me to help.

West, Hannah, and I got scratched to pieces that day, but we also got the cat out of the tree and have been together ever since.

I grin at the memory. Thank goodness for lame ramps and angry cats. "Tell me about it. This funhouse."

West starts to talk, but Hannah puts a hand up to stop him. "Wait! Let me tell her," she says excitedly. "Okay, so what I heard was that these triplets built the funhouse way back in the 1950s. Apparently their parents died when they were like eight years old, and they weren't adopted together. Brutal, right? They grew up separate but found each other again as adults and decided to start building this wacked-out house."

"Wacked-out how?" I ask. "Because we still have every doll I ever owned in our attic. Mom refuses to get rid of them, so they just sit there...staring."

West winces. "Okay, that's creepy, but I think the triplets

still have you beat. They wanted their funhouse to be the most epic one ever built, so no lame stuff like basic mirror mazes. Instead, they built a bunch of complicated secret passages and hid riddles everywhere."

"Like an escape room before there were escape rooms," I whisper.

"Exactly!" He pulls up a picture of the funhouse on his phone and turns the screen to face me.

Whoa.

The building is brick, two stories, and has windows of different shapes and sizes set into its face. Square windows, oval windows, and even a triangular window right in the center. But that's not what surprises me the most. It's the paint. Bright green across the top half and an ocean-like blue on the bottom. Several thick brown stripes start near the roofline and go all the way to the base, where they change shape and become round. A bright yellow circle sits in the lower right.

I narrow my eyes at the puffy, rounded parts of the paint, pinching the picture to make it bigger. The image gets blurry, but not too blurry for me to see that even the front door is strange. It isn't rectangular like a normal door, but instead is shaped and painted like a little house.

I let the picture go back to its normal size and turn West's phone upside down. In the moment before it automatically flips over again, it hits me. Everything is upside down! The green at the top is grass, the blue at the bottom is sky, and the brown lines on either side are trees. I gasp at the door shape, realizing that it's the same shape as the funhouse I'm looking at right now.

West and Hannah start cracking up, probably because my mouth is hanging open like I just saw a spaceship land on my lawn.

"You figured it out, huh?" Hannah asks. "Pretty wild that they had their funhouse painted onto their funhouse."

"Wild," I echo, still trying to make sense of everything I'm looking at. "And upside down too. Hey, is that a slide?"

I tap a fingernail on what looks like a multicolored tube that spirals down from a window on the side of the building. Even following its path with my eyes makes me dizzy. I can't imagine what it would be like to slide down.

West takes his phone back and sets it on the ground in front of us. "Looks like it, but no one really knows much about this place for sure. The triplets never got to open the funhouse because one of them died. The other two were so sad that they never opened it. Eventually they all died, so the funhouse just sits there now...like your dolls."

An unexpected pang of sadness hits me. I don't know anything about these triplets or why they chose to build something odd like a funhouse to begin with. Still, it's kind of awful that they never got to see their dream of opening it come true.

Hannah nods in somber agreement. "It has been abandoned for years."

West picks something off the front of his T-shirt. He's still in the Escape City one and now that the adrenaline has worn off, I realize how truly ugly it is. Like a neon banana. "Yeah. It's definitely more run-down now, but still cool-looking."

He swipes at the screen of his phone, and a different photo of the funhouse comes up. This one shows the windows boarded up and what looks like a big NO TRESPASSING sign on the front door.

"Why would people want to trespass? It's just a broken-down old house now, right?" I ask.

"To find the treasure!" Hannah shouts. "That's the other cool part of the story. The triplets said they hid a treasure somewhere in the funhouse. Who knows? Maybe it's still there."

West shakes his head like the whole idea is ridiculous. I kinda agree with him. What kind of treasure would be hidden in a funhouse, anyway? Coupons for cotton candy? Extra butter on your popcorn? Free face painting?

"The treasure is just a legend. It was probably never real," West says as if reading my mind. "My mom grew up in that town and said most people think the triplets likely made the whole treasure thing up for advertising. You know, to get people interested in their funhouse before it opened."

I think on this for a moment, my mind snagging on the possibilities. In math problems, there are variables— things that can change the way you approach the problem, or the answer. With the funhouse, the triplets are definitely a variable. On one hand, they might have just been trying to hype up their new creation, like West's mom says. That would mean the chances of the treasure being real are probably low. But on the other hand, they might have had a different goal. That would mean the chances of the treasure being real would be higher.

"So, let's pretend there is a treasure still in that funhouse. Who would it belong to?" I ask.

West meets my eyes. "That's the really interesting thing. When the triplets first announced their funhouse, they said the treasure would belong to whoever found it."

Looking back down at his phone, I focus on the board-ed-up windows of the building. The hidden treasure is just a story. People love to tell stories. No matter how wacky the triplets were, I'm positive there's no treasure hidden in the walls of their funhouse.

Right?

Totally. It's a hoax. It has to be. Still, if the treasure is real and it's money, it would change someone's life.

Scratch that. It would change *my* life.

"We should look for it." The words slip out before I can stop them. "The treasure, I mean."

With their wide eyes and parted mouths, my friends look like deer caught in headlights. Not that I blame them. The Deltas don't do anything without thinking it through. Especially risky stuff. Suggesting we sneak into an abandoned funhouse to look for a treasure that might not even exist isn't like me. Then again, it isn't like me to be this desperate and worried either.

"Just hear me out," I continue. "If something doesn't change, the bank is taking our house back. And if we lose our house, Mom said we're going to Michigan to live with Grandma and Grandpa until we 'get back on our feet.'" I use finger quotes on that last part because who knows how long getting back on our feet could take? Weeks? Months? *Years*?

West's jaw drops. "Wait, what? Michigan? You never told us that."

My chin trembles and I feel the sting of tears building again. Fighting them off, I look up at my friends. "I didn't have time to tell you. But there's no choice. We can't afford an apartment here, and my grandparents have enough space."

Silence blankets the room. Hannah breaks it first by slapping her palms against the tops of her legs. "She's right. We're going to the funhouse."

"What?!" West says, raking a hand through his hair. He leaves it standing on end, reminding me of a cartoon character hit by lightning. "Are you guys nuts? Pretty sure since the funhouse isn't open, that would be burglary!"

I hold up a hand hoping he'll calm down. "Only if we get caught."

"No," West starts, jumping up. He paces the length of the room, the legs of his jeans aggressively swishing against each other. "Look at this article! Some guy named William Taters was arrested just last year for trying to break in!"

I laugh before I can stop myself. West gives me a look.

"Sorry. It's just that Taters is a really funny last name."

"Be serious, Sarah. We could get in big, big trouble."

"Or we could save Sarah's house," Hannah interrupts without missing a beat.

Getting up, I cross the room and stand in front of West. "If I move to Michigan, we won't see each other every day. Maybe not at all. No more movie nights, no more bike rides to the ice cream shop—"

"No more escape rooms," Hannah finishes for me.

That gets his attention. West sighs.

"Look. Three hundred and twenty-seven groups have attempted to escape *Lasers and Lava* since it opened. Besides us, only six have beaten the buzzer. That means we had less than point zero one eight percent chance today." I pause and look West in the eyes. "But we did it. We did it because we're good, West. If anyone can get in and out of that funhouse, it's us."

Hannah holds her hands up with her pointer fingers and thumbs touching. But instead of them being in the shape of a heart, they're in the shape of a triangle. "C'mon, Jones. We can't do this without you."

Another sigh.

"Fine," West finally huffs, meeting my eyes with a mischievous smile. "But we're not gonna try this until we've done all the research we can first. I want to know what we're dealing with."

I nod in agreement as the tiniest little sliver of hope blooms inside me.

"Oh," West continues. "And if we end up in jail like that Taters dude, I'm using my one call to cancel the birthday gift I ordered for you."

I smile so hard it hurts. "That's a risk I'm willing to take."

CHAPTER FOUR
THE READER, THE BANKER, THE CABINETMAKER

I agree with West. It makes sense to do some research before we go to the funhouse, but that doesn't keep me from being antsy. It's the same feeling I get about a new escape room, only bigger. Stronger. My brain is itching to get started, to find the treasure.

"Why isn't there more about the funhouse?" West grumbles, easing away from his computer screen and rubbing his eyes. We've been perched on his messy bed, digging through articles and a bag of Twizzlers for over an hour. "I can only find a few articles, and they're so short."

"Same," Hannah says. She's sprawled out on the floor, surrounded by empty Coke cans and a half-eaten box of Sour Patch Kids. She may never sleep again. "I found this one, but it's mostly about how everyone disagreed about what to do with the house for a while."

I lean over and look at the article she has pulled up on her laptop. It's dated September 15, 1962, and features a picture of the funhouse—the same one I saw earlier with the NO TRESPASSING sign. I begin reading aloud. "*Residents of Maplewood have voiced concerns that the seemingly abandoned structure could be hazardous, as well as appealing to bored teens looking for a place to pass time.*"

West laughs. "So, parents were the same back in 1962. Afraid of bored teens."

"Um, have you met my brother? He's a nightmare when he's bored." I snag the Sour Patch Kids and pop two in my mouth, my lips puckering as the sourness hits. "Last year when we couldn't go anywhere during spring break and all his friends were out of town, he tried that whole Coke and Mentos thing. There are still stains on our kitchen ceiling from it!"

Hannah flops backward onto the pillows she's piled up on the rug, clutching her stomach as she laughs. "I remember that! Didn't he try to tell your mom it was a water leak from the bathroom upstairs?"

I nod, a smile finding its way to my lips at the memory of Sean pointing up to a splattered ceiling and pretending he had no idea what happened. Mom didn't buy it for a second.

Of course, it didn't help that some of the Mentos ended up in the flowerpots that sit in our windowsill. Or that he was covered in two liters of sticky brown liquid. Sean's boredom ended pretty fast because she made him clean the whole kitchen the next day.

Looking back at the article, a line pops out at me. "Did you guys notice this article says the funhouse isn't actually *in* Maplewood? It's about a mile outside the city limits."

"Seems like a strange place to build a funhouse," Hannah says. "Don't businesses want to be in busy areas, so they get more customers?"

"I guess. I never really thought about it," I admit. Now that Hannah brings it up though, it does seem weird. Not that there's anything about this funhouse so far that isn't.

"Wait, check this out," West says, angling his computer screen toward us. It's a photo. Three men in suits are standing side by side. They all wear the same small round glasses and even the same curious expression. They look like adults, but young adults. Twentysomething maybe. "This is them, right? The triplets?"

I squint as I look from one face to the next. They really are identical.

Hannah crawls closer to him and clicks on the link. The article opens. "Hans, Stefan, and Karl Stein."

"Those are German names, aren't they?" West asks no one in particular. "My mom's side of the family came from Germany, and her great grandpa's name was Hans."

"Yup!" Hannah answers, tapping her finger on a paragraph further down in the article. "Says here that the triplets were born in the United States, but their parents emigrated from Germany in 1926 right after they got married."

That's when the article takes a dark turn. Even though I was expecting it, my heart squeezes uncomfortably. "The parents died in a car accident in 1934. Hans, Stefan, and Karl were eight."

Hannah's mouth is turned down. "That's so sad."

It is sad. Even though Sean makes me nuts sometimes, I can't imagine if something happened to both of our parents, and we were split up. Things are far from perfect right now, but at least we're still together.

"I wonder why they had to be split up." I don't even realize I've said it out loud until West answers. "Seems like they should've been adopted together."

"Wasn't that during the Great Depression though?" West asks. "I bet people didn't have money to adopt one kid. Three was probably impossible."

Ugh. Money. Why is it so hard for people to get as much as they need? Right now, my parents could never adopt another kid even if they wanted to. Another person to feed, another person who needs clothes and school supplies. We can't even pay for our house. I bet the triplets were even more scared than I am now.

"The Second World War started a few years later too." he adds. "I remember learning about it last year and thinking that the thirties and forties seemed like a tough time to be alive. I bet it was an even worse time to be an orphan."

"But they eventually got adopted, right?" Hannah asks.

I scroll down, my throat thick with discomfort. "Yeah. But it took years, and they all went to different homes."

"Says here that they didn't find each other again until they were in their twenties." West has given up on getting his laptop back from Hannah and has opened the article on his phone. "Hans was taken in by a family who owned a cabinet-making business. And Stefan"—he pauses to keep scrolling—"it looks like he went on to college. Must've studied math or something because he became a banker."

"What about Karl?" I prompt. "Does it say what he did?"

"*There are no records of Karl Stein graduating from college,*" West reads aloud. "*But evidence suggests the young man may have briefly studied literature before taking a job at a local bookstore.*"

I run over the new information in my head the same way

I'd replay clues in an escape room. It's interesting, but I'm not sure how any of it helps us. Just when I think we've wasted the past two hours of our Sunday, Hannah gasps.

"What?" I ask, craning my neck to see the computer screen.

"It's a video about someone who tried to find the treasure!" She clicks a few buttons and waits for West to join us on the floor before clicking Play. A young man in a Hawaiian print T-shirt is being loaded into the back of a police car. He's got floppy brown hair that's way too long, neon blue sunglasses, and tight jeans rolled up at the ankles. Definitely an old video. No one I know would be caught dead looking like this.

The camera turns to a woman with similarly shaggy hair and comically large glasses. She pushes them up her nose and brings a microphone to her mouth.

"Welcome back, Maplewood. I'm Janet Erikson report-ing from Stagecoach Road, where yet another trespasser has just been detained by police for attempting to find the so-called Triplet Treasure in the run-down structure you see behind me. I've been asked to remind all of our viewers that, despite the original creators' apparent invitation to search for the rumored treasure, this building is strictly off-limits. We do not know the condition of the interior, and ownership is still in question."

The video ends as the police car drives off with the man inside.

"'Ownership is still in question'?" West repeats. "How is that possible? This video is dated March of 1988. How were they confused about who owned the funhouse over thirty years after the triplets stopped building it?"

I shrug. There's tension between my shoulder blades and a dull ache in my head now. This is way more confusing than I expected it to be. "The triplets have to own it, right? I mean, they're the ones who challenged people to find the treasure. You can't hide a treasure in a place that doesn't belong to you and invite people in to find it. They'd be trespassing."

There *is* a big NO TRESPASSING sign on the door. Still, there isn't any evidence that the triplets ever sold the funhouse. Shouldn't that mean they still own it, or can you not own things anymore after you die?

West and Hannah are quiet. The end of the video is still frozen on screen.

"Hey...which triplet"—I hesitate, feeling uncomfortable— "which one *died*?"

"Stefan," West answers matter-of-factly. "There's an obituary for him that says he was only twenty-eight."

Twenty-eight? So much tragedy in one family. I try to brush it off, but my thoughts keep coming back to my own family. My mom, who never gets enough sleep. My brother, who isn't excited about college because of money, even though he should be. And then there's Dad. The dad who went from never being able to sit still to being still *all* the time. We need some good news soon.

We need that treasure.

"So, Stefan probably left his third of the funhouse to Karl and Hans," I say, working the situation through in my head. "They were sad, so they decided not to open it, and instead hid money in the walls and challenged everyone in town to find it?"

"Treasure," Hannah corrects. "Could be jewels or something. Gold coins."

"They weren't pirates, Hannah," I say with a laugh.

West's caterpillar eyebrows are back. "Guess this makes sense, but if the triplets actually wanted people to search for whatever they hid in the walls, why is it all boarded up like this?"

It's a great question. One I can't answer right now. The triplets have all been gone for years though. Maybe they never expected the house to end up like this.

Still scrolling, West shakes his head sadly. "It looks like Hans and Karl died back in the nineties. One in 1994 and one in 1998. Doesn't say what they died from."

"Are there any interviews with them from back then? Did

they talk about the funhouse at all?" I ask, leaning over to see his screen.

"Not once. No interviews, nothing." He sets his phone down with a sigh. "I don't get it. They built this amazing house and then pretty much pretended it didn't exist."

"They were probably too sad to do anything else," I say. Sometimes when I see things I used to do with Dad, I feel that way. Like the storage tub of frisbees and Nerf footballs in the basement, which we used to pull out on hot summer days. Dad is here, but also *not* here, so seeing that box makes me uncomfortable, like I don't want to do any of that stuff if he can't do it with me. Maybe it was the same for Hans and Karl. Without Stefan, the funhouse just might not have been fun anymore.

"Guys, the man they showed being taken away by police in that video wasn't a nobody," Hannah says suddenly, her voice oddly hushed.

"Was it William Taters?" West asks.

She shakes her head. "No. It was a guy named Arthur, or Art, Conley. He had a television show called *Art Matters*. Looks like he went all over the country exploring different types of art. He wanted to use the funhouse in one of his episodes because it's so unique, but he couldn't get past the first room."

"So?" I ask. "It's not like he was good at escape rooms and still failed, you know?"

"Yeah, but he was kinda famous. He had a TV show and they still arrested him!"

Now I see what she's getting at. The risk isn't just whether we can finish the house or not; it's if we get caught trying. If the police were willing to arrest a man who had his own show, what will they do to us?

Suddenly I don't feel so good. I'm expecting West to chime in now, to tell us this is a horrible idea, and we need to forget all about it, but he doesn't. Instead, he takes a deep breath, closes his laptop, and looks me straight in the eyes.

"Well, we'll just have to be smarter and faster than William Taters *and* Art Conley, then."

CHAPTER FIVE
CHUCK E. CHEESE AND COLD FEET

Figuring out how to take the train wasn't as hard as I thought it would be. West bought the tickets online, and Hannah used her Uber account to get us to the station. Then all three of us told our parents we were tackling a new escape room today. It's not a full lie, really. Just a baby one. The funhouse isn't exactly an escape room, but, hey, it has rooms and we'll be trying to escape!

"I really hope this wasn't a mistake," West mutters, his eyes trained on the blur of trees rolling past.

"It wasn't. I can already tell." Hannah unwraps a piece of gum and sticks it in her mouth. It's the third since our train left the station five minutes ago.

"And how can you tell that?" I ask with a laugh.

She snaps a bubble in my face with a grin. "Because I have a feeling. A good one!"

I smile even though I have a feeling too, and it's not exactly good. It's more like a *butterflies trying to kill each other in my stomach* feeling.

When the train finally stops at the station, I realize how nervous I am. My legs feel rubbery, and my heart is beating fast. Truth is, not knowing any odds for something like this is scaring me. What are our chances of getting in? No clue. What are our chances of getting caught? Again, no clue.

Will we discover the treasure doesn't even exist?

A sigh escapes me. West tosses his backpack over a shoulder, scowling. "Was that an *I'm getting cold feet* sigh?"

"Not just cold. Frigid," I admit. "Is this stupid?"

A gentle smile fills his face. "It's never stupid to want to help. I know how hard things have been for you guys, and I'd probably do the same thing."

Laughing, I shake my head. "Liar."

"Fine," he says with a deep belly laugh of his own. "I wouldn't. But I think it's cool of you. Really."

"Let's hope you're still saying that at the end of today. And not from behind bars." The butterflies start thrashing again. "I looked up William Taters. He tried to pry the front door off its hinges!"

West makes a choking sound. "We aren't going to pry the door off."

"We aren't going to get arrested either. Haven't you guys seen any heist movies before?" Hannah asks, shoving a chunk of hair behind her ear. "They always put together a team of the most qualified people. That's us. Seriously. We got this!"

She spins a full circle, then crosses her arms over her chest. "But we have to find it first. Do you guys know which direction it is? I see some houses, a gas station, and"—she squints—"a Chuck E. Cheese."

Gross. The last time I was in one of those places a kid threw up in the ball pit.

"According to Maps, it's one point four miles from here." West points down the street, then glances back down at his phone. "We need to head that way."

I focus on the scenery as we walk. Maplewood isn't half-bad. The houses are small but nice, and every yard we pass has flowers lining the sidewalk. It's not that different from Park Glen where West, Hannah, and I live. The only difference? Maplewood has the Triplet Treasure. At least I hope it does. Otherwise today is going to be a bigger bust than the first two times we tried to win *Lasers and Lava*.

The street begins to look less and less city-like. There

are more trees than buildings, and eventually, fields line both sides. Gravel crunches beneath my ratty sneakers, and even though it's still morning, the sun is warm. Spring in Illinois is pretty nice actually. You usually start your day with a jacket on but end it in a T-shirt.

Hopefully today we end with a treasure in our hands. Big, small, I don't care. As long as it pays that giant stack of bills, I'll be happy.

"We're getting close, guys," West says, watching the little blue dot on his phone screen. Since it's moving farther and farther away from town, I'm guessing it's us.

"Good, because this feels farther than one point four miles," Hannah grumbles. "And I keep getting rocks in my shoes."

It also feels a *little* scary. I've never lived in the country before, and even though this isn't very far outside town, it feels like it is. We haven't seen any people or cars or...well, anything except fields since we walked past the city limit sign.

We continue on for another five minutes or so before something big and bright takes shape in the distance.

The funhouse.

"Sarah?" West says, prodding me in the arm. "You okay?"

"Yeah," I answer, realizing I stopped walking. "Just nervous. There's so much that could go wrong."

"None of it will. We prepared. Like Hannah said, we got this."

I swallow hard and look back the way we came. The city limit sign is so far away I can't see it anymore, can't see anything but wide-open fields and a long stretch of dusty road. This is all so different from the normal escape rooms we do. Usually, we're in a waiting room now, and the building is buzzing with excited people. Sometimes you can even hear them through the walls as they attempt their own room, cheering or moaning. Once we even heard something break, and I'm pretty sure that group got kicked out for trying a little *too* hard to escape.

I have a feeling we aren't going to hear anything out here. Well, maybe a crow or a tractor.

Taking a steadying breath, I start walking again. I'm nervous, but I have to believe Hannah and West are right.

We got this.

CHAPTER SIX

FORTUNE FAVORS THE BOLD

The funhouse is every bit as bright and bizarre as I expected it to be. The slide snakes down from the roof at a wild angle and ends in a patch of overgrown weeds. I follow it with my eyes up to the second floor where it goes straight into the side of the building. Interesting. The triplets must have planned for that to be a possible exit. Maybe even the exit you'd go through if you completed the house. I imagine sliding down it with a sack of gold or money in my lap and grin.

Looking back down, I notice that just like in the photo, the windows are boarded up and a NO TRESPASSING sign is tacked to the front door. I scan the area, noticing that there are two farmhouses nearby. They're far enough away that a lot of people wouldn't consider them neighbors, but out here in the country, things are probably different.

The funhouse itself sits in the middle of an empty field. Tall, scratchy prairie grass has grown up all around it, and there's a scattering of wildflowers here and there. This is good. Less houses means less eyes, and less eyes means less chances to get caught like that dingbat William Taters. Oh, and Art whatever his name was. Can't forget him and his horrible outfit.

"I think we should go around the back of the house first. Look for a way in that isn't so obvious," West says.

Hannah laughs. "Obvious to who? Look around, West. We're in the middle of nowhere."

His eyebrows are bunched together so tightly that they remind me of a caterpillar. "This isn't the middle of nowhere. There are two farms right there, and one of them has a truck in the driveway. Someone is home for sure."

I shudder at the thought that they could be watching us already. Maybe they have binoculars or just really good eyesight. The idea makes me want to drop into the tall grass and start army crawling.

"We need to watch out for cameras too," West adds. "Don't know if they have any on this place but we can't be too careful."

We quickly jog into the side yard. Hannah looks up and down the building. "There are definitely no cameras on this side. But there's also no side door, and the windows are too high to reach."

I follow her gaze up to the first set of windows. An oval one and a very skinny rectangular one. They look so odd next to each other. Like lollipops with grasshoppers inside. Some things just don't go together.

As my eyes glide back down, I notice something else. A breeze shifts the bushes, giving me a brief glimpse of a different color set into blue bricks. Red, maybe? I narrow my eyes on the spot. The wind blows again, and I inhale with excitement. *Yes.* There's something there.

Walking over, I use one arm to hold the bush branches to the side so I can get a better view of the...whatever it is.

"What is that?" Hannah asks, looking over my shoulder.

West crowds in and helps me hold the bush out of the way. "Weird. Is that a picture?"

It *is* a picture—a really odd one. It's small and square, with a faded image in the center. A wishbone. The paint is cracked and chipped off in places, and it's set inside a thick black frame. It looks old, almost older than something from the 1950s.

"Why would they decorate here, behind the bushes where no one can see the picture anyway?" Hannah muses.

"They wouldn't," I say, my heart thumping faster. Rule

number one of escape rooms: if something looks out of place, it's probably important.

West gestures for Hannah to grab the branches in my way and hold them to the side like the other half of a curtain. Then I crawl through the gap in the shrubbery and grip the picture frame. At first it doesn't budge. After a few attempts to pull it, I realize my mistake. It doesn't pull; it twists.

Rotating the picture to the left like a steering wheel, I gasp at the sound it makes. It's metallic and thick and comes from somewhere inside the wall.

"Did you hear that? Guys. There has to be something here." I press on the bricks frantically, adrenaline coursing through me. "That sounded exactly like the deadbolt on our front door being unlocked!"

West and Hannah begin barking out orders. "Press there!" "Pull the frame!" "Kick that!" "Use two hands!"

I do it all, but nothing works.

"Now what?" Hannah asks. "We could go back to plan A and see if we can get in through the back."

I collapse against the wall, panting in defeat. Just then, something rains down over my head and shoulders. Bending down, I immediately start shaking out my curls. With my luck it's probably a bunch of baby spiders.

"What the?" White flecks fall out of my hair and speckle the dirt.

When I look up, Hannah's mouth is hanging open, her stale gum teetering dangerously. And West is grinning.

West only grins like that when we're about to win.

Spinning around, I see what they're gaping at. Cracks have formed between some of the bricks, creating a rectangular outline. Excited, I put both hands against the wall and shove. The cracks widen just enough for me to tell that the rectangle outline is in the shape of something familiar and very, very exciting.

A door!

My heart skips a beat. Secret passages are one of my favorite things about escape rooms because sometimes they're a shortcut. A way to get to the good stuff faster. Maybe that's why this is here. Maybe the triplets created a secret passage that will get us closer to the treasure quicker.

That is, if it exists.

"The pressure of you leaning on the wall must have done that," West says, running a finger over the crack closest to him. He wrestles the bush out of the way once more. "Can you do it again?"

Nodding, I lean against the bricks. They feel cool against my flushed skin, but other than getting another small dusting of powder, nothing happens.

"I don't think I'm strong enough. Let's all try. Get in here, West!"

Still holding the branches, Hannah begins wading through the tangle of bushes to stand at my side. West crawls in after her. Branches slap and claw at our skin, but we don't care. We're close. I can feel it. Sweat slips into my eye as we press our bodies into the bricks as hard as possible.

Ever so slowly, the bricks begin to shift inward. There's a scraping sound as they give way. We keep pushing, grunting, and pressing with all our strength until the wall stops moving.

A musty smell hits my nose.

The smell of victory.

The entire door shape has been indented into the wall, leaving about three feet open on either side. Cobwebs hang across the entrance. Just enough sunlight streams in to light up the floor. It's covered with a thick layer of dust.

"Told you," Hannah says, rubbing her hands together like a cartoon villain. "We're the best. If we were trying to steal a priceless gem or artifact right now, we'd so be going home with it."

"Will you stop talking about stealing stuff? You're making me more nervous," West says through gritted teeth. He's still wrestling with the bush, his eyes darting around nervously.

Hannah snaps one final bubble, then tosses her gum into the bushes. "Relax. It's going to be a lot harder to find the treasure if you have a heart attack and we have to carry you through."

While my friends continue to squabble, I sweep some of the dust aside with my sneaker. There are tiles beneath, colorful ones. Flipping on my cell phone light, I shine it down, noticing that it's a mosaic with words in the center.

AUDENTIS FORTUNA IUVAT.

Hannah and West go quiet as they stare down at it with me.

"Fortune favors the bold," West breathes out.

I blink at him, puzzled. "Um, what language even is that, and how do you know how to read it?"

He laughs. "It's Latin. I don't know how to read it; I just know that phrase. Saw it in a commercial once."

Ah. Of course, he saw it in a commercial. It was probably years ago, and because of his freakishly good memory, he's never forgotten it.

I look back down at the words peeking through the dust and shiver. Out of all the things this mosaic could say, this might be the worst. I'm not bold. I'm not even brave. Not normally.

"We should get in before anyone at those farmhouses sees us," West says, nudging me forward. I stumble into the dark, wipe the cobwebs from my face, and tell myself to be happy. We're officially in the house, and that means whatever our odds are, they just went up.

CHAPTER SEVEN
A BIG TOP ENTRANCE

The wall grinds closed again, leaving us in darkness. My eyes struggle to adjust, and my nose twitches with the beginning of a sneeze.

So. Much. Dust.

I stumble over what sounds like an army of plastic water bottles on the floor. The noise makes my heart sink. Water bottles on the floor means we aren't the first people to make it into this room. Not that I expected us to be. Good ol' Arthur Conley is proof. I bet a lot of people have tried to find the treasure before getting caught. Or failing.

We are *not* going to fail.

West's cell phone light flicks on. Then Hannah's. I shield my eyes until they're used to the glare, then look around.

"Wow," Hannah says breathlessly. "This is..."

"Insane," I finish for her. Now that my eyes are finally working again, I'm in awe. Since we came through the wall instead of a normal front door, I expected us to be standing in a dirty old mudroom or something. I was wrong. The space is huge! The walls are striped red and white, and the ceiling is angled so that it comes to a point in the center. Small multicolored flags are strung overhead in a zigzag pattern. I can't help but smile at the shape. *Triangles*. If I believed in signs or luck or any of that stuff, I'd be thrilled right now.

"It's a circus tent!" Hannah exclaims, twirling in a circle.

My mouth hangs open as I take it all in. Hannah is right. The way the stripes curve and the ceiling slopes *does* make the room look like the inside of a circus tent! It's probably one of the best illusions I've ever seen.

I'm trying to calculate how tall the ceiling actually is when a crash rings out.

"Ow!" West shouts. "My leg!"

Spinning around to shine my light in West's direction, I gasp. He's sitting on the floor, face twisted in a grimace. One leg is bent at the knee in front of him, but his left foot is stuck down in the floor. Jagged wooden planks are sticking out around his ankle like teeth trying to swallow him whole.

I scramble to his side with Hannah and begin prying the

broken wooden planks as far away from his leg as possible. "What happened?"

West manages a chuckle. "Um, I took a step?"

Hannah helps him navigate out of the hole while I keep the wood out of the way. Other than a few scrapes and scratches, West's ankle looks okay. Still, my stomach is flip-flopping. I shine my flashlight into the hole, shuddering. It's too dark to see much but shards of wood and bits of other materials. I swallow hard. If that had happened on the second floor, could West have fallen through?

"I don't know, guys," I say, sucking in a shaky breath. "That was scary. Maybe this house isn't safe."

"I'm fine," West says, pushing his jeans back down over his ankle. "It's not like a horde of killer bees or carnivorous rats came at me. It's a few scrapes."

"He's right, Sarah. Remember that time I hurt my finger in that escape room where we had to get out of those prison cells?" Hannah asks. "We didn't quit then, and we aren't quitting now."

West levels an entertained look in her direction. "To be fair, that was a splinter, Hannah. I was just half eaten by the floor. Little different!"

"Thought you said it was just a scratch!" she retorts, folding her arms over her chest.

"Stop it!" I hiss. "Seriously, you guys."

I expect one of them to say something snarky back, but instead they're just staring at me. Or rather, *behind* me. Hannah's eyes widen, and West opens his mouth to speak but can't seem to get the words out.

Whirling around, I see what they're focused on.

A clown.

The doll is around two feet tall and sitting on a shelf set into the wall. It has a shiny plastic face. The eyes are glassy, and the colorfully striped jumpsuit he's wearing is partially torn, like someone tried to remove it. Between the ripped clothing and the bits of plastic peeling off its face here and there, it isn't the most comforting clown I've ever seen.

Hannah shudders beside me. "Isn't this supposed to be a funhouse? Because that's not fun."

"Yeah, it's a little creepy." I point at the big red button next to it. "Wh-what do you think that does?"

"I think it gives the clown permission to bite the person who pushed it," West answers with a laugh. "Seriously, though—don't push it."

Pffft. Doesn't West know that telling me not to push it only makes me want to push it more? He's right though. As much as I want to know what it does, I shouldn't push it until I'm certain. It could open a trapdoor or do something totally unrelated to the clown. Escape rooms are great at disguising things. So far, this funhouse isn't much different than one.

I take a step back, losing my balance when the clown suddenly springs forward. Hitting the floor with a thud, I scramble away. The clown dangles out from the wall on a long spring. There's a sound too. A warped, mechanical sound.

A laugh.

West and Hannah are laughing too. Meanwhile, I'm rubbing at my sore tailbone and wondering how I set off the clown without touching the button.

"What a great trick. There must be another trigger for it," Hannah says. "Maybe it's motion activated? Like doors?"

"Did they even have motion-activated stuff in the fifties?" West poses.

"I have no idea, but I did something to make that *thing* move." I brush off my pants and stick out my tongue at the clown. "Forget it for now. If we're going to do this, then we need to get moving before someone realizes we're in here." I look from West to Hannah, hoping they can tell how serious I am, even without seeing me that well. "Or we'll end up like William Taters."

West fights off a smile. Apparently, I'm not the only one who thinks that last name is hilarious. "All right. All right. Let's do this, Deltas." He takes another look around the space and sighs. "It really sucks that we aren't the first people to get into this room."

"I know." I examine a shattered mirror on the wall. There are three of them, the long wavy kind that distort your body. This one is so broken that the only thing I can see is how big my head looks. Like a bowling ball sitting on top of a toothpick.

"I wonder how many people have been in here and how far they got," I say.

"Well, they made it far enough to find another door," West answers. "Check this out."

The door he's pointing at is small, only about three feet tall. There's no doorknob on it, and three oddly shaped locks run up and down the edge. A wishbone is carved into the center of the wood.

"Same symbol we saw on the wall outside. It must be important." West looks from the door to Hannah and me. "Wishbones mean luck, right?"

"I think so. Maybe it's a clue?" I think back to the wishbone on the wall outside and how we couldn't understand why someone would decorate behind the bushes. Suddenly it hits me. "Yes! Think about it—we almost didn't see that little picture. The only reason I did is because the wind blew and moved the bushes."

"Luck," West whispers.

"Exactly."

Hannah crouches next to the door, laughing. "We would have to crawl through this thing. It kinda reminds me of something from *Alice in Wonderland*."

"Or *Willy Wonka*," I add with a snort. I never did like that movie. It's supposed to be magical or fun or whatever, but really, it's just plain old creepy. Now that I think about it though, the triplets were a little creepy. I remember the picture of them we discovered before we came here. They were wearing the same outfit. I've seen little kids do that, but adults? Must've been their thing, like the way they marketed themselves.

My eyes stop on a warped spot in the floor a few feet away. "Hey, what is that?"

"Huh," Hannah scampers over to the area where the wood is curved upward and blows away the dust. "The wood is bumpy here."

The image of West's foot stuck in the floor pops into my head. "Don't step on it!"

"I won't. Sheesh." Hannah's face wrinkles at me. "All I was going to say is that this happened at my house next to our sliding glass doors. Mom said it was because water got in and messed up the wood."

West and I squat down beside her. He looks from the

floor to the ceiling. "Doesn't look like any water came in though. Wouldn't we see stains or something?"

Keeping my distance, I reach out and gently press on the wood. There's a clicking sound, then the same grinding we heard when the door in the wall closed. A panel of the same red and white striped wallpaper slowly glides over the small door until it's hidden from sight.

Hannah gasps. "A button!"

"A button in the floor," I add, looking back across the room at the clown dangling from the wall. "That must've been how I triggered the clown too! I stepped on a hidden button!"

"So, it *was* luck!" West says. "Whoever walked over here must've stepped on that spot in the floor and revealed the hidden door by accident."

I nod, impressed with the triplets for hiding that door so well. Once the panel is fully in place, it's truly invisible. I'm also impressed with us. Normally, the escape rooms we do are reset before we come in. Everything is back in its original place and ready for us. Not here, though. No one has reset anything ever, which means we're stuck trying to figure out the clues backward.

"Odds are good that whoever found that door probably also found the key." I say, wishing we could just pry the door open.

Looking back at the door, I imagine myself unlocking it and crawling through, key lodged in my sweaty palms as it slides closed behind me. "I bet the door closed behind them just like that wall closed behind us."

"Which means we can't use this door," West adds, scowling. "I'm sure they took the key with them. We would."

"True. But there could be another key in here to it." I press on the floor again. The panel slides away, revealing the door a second time. "Yes! There are three locks, so maybe that means there are three keys?"

West takes the backpack from his shoulder and opens it, revealing a pile of mini flashlights. "Before we start looking for other keys, we should turn our cell phone lights off, guys. They'll run down our batteries."

Hannah waves her phone in his direction. "Um, unfortunately I don't think that's going to matter much. No signal anyway."

Noooooo. I turn my phone light off and check the bars. They're flatter than the cardboard-like pancakes my brother makes on the weekends. "Gah! Not even one bar? This is bad. How will we know if anyone is looking for us?"

West looks unnerved. "We won't. But we all used the same story, right? That we were going downtown to do a new escape room and we would have to put our phones in the bucket?"

Hannah and I nod.

"Okay, good. Then our parents won't get suspicious if they can't reach us. Only thing is, it's a little scary that we can't call for help if we need it."

I take a shaky breath, worry creeping back in. Our phones not working is a surprise, and not a good one. In a normal escape room, we can quit anytime. Usually someone is monitoring us by camera so if one of us gets sick or hurt we can just say, "Let us out." Here we don't have that option. And now without phones, we don't have *any* option.

Does this change our odds of finding the treasure? Probably not. But it definitely changes our odds of getting caught...or worse.

CHAPTER EIGHT

THE RULE OF THREES

"We need to move fast," I say, mostly to keep myself focused. "The treasure obviously isn't going to be in this room. That would be too easy. That means we need to either find a key that will let us through that door, *or* a different door."

"Agreed," West says. "A lot of escape rooms have multiple exits into the next room."

Hannah marches across the room to a narrow metal staircase in the corner. "I'll look up here."

She takes a few steps up, stopping when I reach through the bars and snag her leg. "Wait. We need to stick together. There could be trapdoors in here. We can't risk getting separated," I glance back at the hole in the floor. "Or hurt."

"Besides," West cranes his neck to look at the ceiling. "This *definitely* isn't the way up. Look."

I follow his line of sight until I see what he's looking at. The staircase reaches the ceiling, then just...stops.

"A stairway that goes nowhere? Why would they do that?" Hannah asks, coming back down the steps with a huff.

"To throw us off," I mutter. "Funhouses are supposed to be confusing and this"—I wave my arms at the strange *nowhere to go* staircase—"this is confusing."

Normally I love escape rooms. They take my mind off the real world and all the bad things waiting for me at home. This house is different. I'm not just doing it for fun. I'm doing it for my mom. For Dad and Sean.

"The triplets were tricky," West says. "But not too tricky for the Deltas. Here's the plan: Hannah and I will look for other hidden doors. Sarah, you work on finding another key. Deal?"

I nod and shake off my nerves. If we have any hope of finding this treasure, we need to focus. *I* need to focus.

West immediately begins pounding at the wall. *Thump, thump, thump-thump-thump.*

I know that pounding. It's a system we call "the pattern." Back when we first started doing escape rooms together, we missed a lot of important clues because our search was too chaotic and haphazard. So we got organized and created our own system. We've used it to look for all kinds of hollow spaces and secret passages.

West starts up as high as he can reach and pounds his fists on the wall all the way down to the floor, then scoots over a foot and does the same thing. Hannah follows his lead and starts at the opposite end of the wall so they will eventually meet in the middle. It isn't always fast, but it's fool-proof. One of us always comes across a section of wall that sounds different...empty. And that's it. That's the clue.

I take a step back from the scene and think through my plan. How am I going to find hidden keys in a room that has already been so picked over?

By thinking differently. The William Taters and Arthur Conleys of the world may have gotten in, but that doesn't mean they had the skills to get far. The Deltas do though. Letting my eyes flutter closed, I imagine the room when it was brand new. Gleaming floors, bright red and white walls instead of fading wallpaper. Where would the triplets have hidden another key? Where would I have hidden it if I created this funhouse? My mind snaps back to the wallpaper. They used the striped pattern to hide one of the doors. Maybe they could have used it to hide keys as well!

"West, I need your backpack," I say, rushing to his side.

West stops pounding on the wall and shrugs it off his shoulders. Setting it on the ground, he waves his hands at the dust that billows up. "What's wrong? Your batteries aren't low already, are they?"

"No. Not that. When do you think black lights were invented?"

His jaw twitches as he thinks. "No clue. Why?"

"Because if this funhouse was built in the fifties, they might not have had fluorescent paint yet. But if they did..."

West's eyes widen. "Then they could have used it to camouflage doors!"

"Or keys!" I add. My palms get sweaty with the idea.

I dig around in West's bag until I find what I'm looking for. Our special flashlight. Most escape rooms provide them, but I think they're so cool that I convinced West and Hannah to chip in with me and buy one of our own. Instead of shining a normal beam of light, these flashlights shine ultraviolet light. And ultraviolet light is excellent at revealing hidden objects.

Starting on the other side of the room, I slowly shine the UV flashlight over the walls, stopping to examine anything that sticks out. There are a few random stains that show up (gross) and a splatter that looks exactly like someone sneezed on the wall (grosser). It's the third thing I find that takes my breath away.

The outline of a key.

The key is nailed to the center of a red stripe. It shows up bright purple, but when I turn the ultraviolet light off, it blends in perfectly with the red. No wonder no one has found it yet! Most people don't carry around UV flashlights. Thank goodness the Deltas aren't most people.

Setting the flashlight on the floor, I grasp the key and wiggle it until the nail is loose. Then I pull it off the wall, marveling at the red paint they used to camouflage it.

West is right. The triplets were tricky!

I open my mouth to yell about having found the key, but Hannah erupts into a squeal. She's jumping around so excitedly that her hair flops over her face. I laugh as I jog in her direction. Maybe in another life she was a sheepdog.

"What? What is it?" West asks.

"Look," she says, her breath coming out in shallow pants. "I was pounding on the wall when I must've randomly hit another button because *this* opened." She taps her sneakered toe next to a section of wood that's missing. Just below the surface is another door, bigger than the Willy Wonka one but still barely large enough for a human to fit through.

Snaking an arm around Hannah's shoulders, I give her an excited squeeze. "I can't believe you found it so fast!"

Hannah grins. It's dazzling, that smile. Even on my worst days when everything is going wrong with Dad, Mom is panicking about bills, and Sean is stressed about college applications, Hannah and her smile make me feel better. Today her smile makes me feel confident, like we might actually be able to do this.

West drops down onto all fours to examine the door. Hannah does the same. My eyes glide over it, noticing that it has hinges on one side and a grab-type handle on the other. *Like a cabinet*, I think, remembering what West said about one of the triplets being adopted by a family who owned a cabinetmaking business. Hans. I run a finger over the wood. It's still smooth and pretty after all these years. Maybe he had something to do with that. The thought is oddly comforting.

"Different symbol," Hannah says, blowing a puff of air onto the door to clear the dirt. "What is that?"

"Not a wishbone, that's for sure. It looks like a book, maybe?" I answer.

West squints at it. "No, not a book. I think it's a deck of cards." He shines the regular flashlight directly on the symbol. I can't make out all the tiny images, but I can see one for sure—the Queen of Hearts.

Interesting. If the wishbone we saw before was meant to signify luck, then what would a deck of cards mean? I add both the wishbone and the deck of cards to the notes I'm taking in my head. Not that I need to with West and his freakishly good memory. I just feel better if more than one of us is keeping track of important details. Hannah is great at a lot of things, like finding hidden buttons and doors, but details isn't really one of them.

Opening my palm, I hold out the key I found hidden on the other side of the room. Hannah shrieks.

"Try it," West says, his voice cracking with excitement.

With shaking hands, I line the key up with the first lock on the door. It won't go in. Second lock, same. Third lock, the key will go in, but it won't turn. I fight the urge to throw it across the room. What good is a key if we don't have the matching door?

"We have to be missing something," I think out loud.

My eyes glide from the triangle flags dangling above us, to the broken mirrors, then over to the locks on the doors we've found. That's when it hits me... Everything in this room is in groups of three!

Three mirrors.

Three locks.

Three sides on the triangles.

Even the triplets themselves were in threes!

"Oh my gosh! They used the rule of threes," I say.

West's face is pinched like he's trying to recall a formula. "Is that a math thing?"

"Not exactly. I learned about it in English. Basically, the idea is that things are more memorable if it's in a group of three. Like 'Three Blind Mice,' or 'Goldilocks and the Three Bears,' or even 'The Three Little Pigs'! Look around this room. *Everything* is in threes. The mirrors, the locks, everything! That means since my key doesn't work on either of the two doors we've found so far, there should be one more door hidden in this room!"

"Yes!" Hannah jumps up and dusts off her kneecaps. "We use that in dance too. I mean, we used to." She goes quiet for a moment, the way she always does when she talks about dance, then lifts her chin. "Our instructor always said that three movements back to back are more satisfying for the audience!"

Looking at my friends, their eyes lit with excitement, I realize that the locks, doors, mirrors, and flags aren't the only things following the rule of threes. We are too. The Deltas. I stand up and clap the dust from my palms, an odd feeling of calm settling over me. I know the triplets probably didn't care who found their treasure, but part of me is excited at the thought that this could be the best clue we've found so far. Maybe, just maybe, this funhouse has been waiting...for *us*.

CHAPTER NINE
DELTAS DON'T GIVE UP

Ten minutes later and I'm blinking at a fresh set of locks. I can't believe we found the third door!

West steps back and rubs his hand over his jawline. "Huh. Not the door I was expecting."

Same. The door is tiny and rectangular, more like a safe built into the wall than anything. Forget crawling; to get through this one we'd have to shrink!

Please let this be something. Please, please, please.

With a deep breath, I stick the key in the first lock and twist.

There's a soft clink followed by a gasp from West as the door springs open. A rope lies coiled up inside.

At first, I'm thrilled. After all these years and all the

stupid William Taters of the world, the Deltas are the first people to open this door and find the rope! I let the thought settle in, feeling proud. Yes, we've spent more time in this room than I wanted to, at least a half hour, but it was worth it for this moment.

West shakes my shoulder, pulling me from my thoughts. "Hey. Earth to Sarah?"

"Sorry. Just spaced out for a second." I turn the rope over in my hands. It's thick and has an odd fastener on one end, like the triplets expected us to hook it to something.

But what?

"What could they have given this to us for?" Hannah thinks out loud.

West examines the metal clamp at the end of the rope. "Pulling something, maybe?"

Looking around the room, I shrug. "There's nothing in here to pull unless we're supposed to move the table."

West crosses to the table, dodging the hole in the floor on his way. He grips the corner and gently lifts until the bottom of the leg is off the floor. "I don't think that's it. The table is really light. Even if there was only one of us instead of three, I can't imagine anyone needing a rope to move it."

Panic begins to seep in. I swing my flashlight beam from end to end of the room, wondering what we're missing.

The rope is heavy-duty. I examine it one more time, noticing that the fastener on the end is like a latch that can be open or closed. Sean went through a rock–climbing phase, and this looks a lot like the clamps they used to secure harnesses and stuff.

"Hey! There's something else in here," Hannah shoves her hand in the space where we found the rope. When she pulls it back out, she's holding a piece of paper.

I shine my light on her hands as she begins unfolding it. "What does it say?"

Hannah begins to read out loud. "*He floats through the air with the greatest of ease, the daring young man on the—*" She stops reading, her eyes flickering with shock.

"On the what?" West says, crowding her. "Finish it, Hannah!"

"*On the flying trapeze.*" Hannah finally spits out. Her voice cracks on the word *trapeze*.

"Flying trapeze?" I croak, my palms growing clammy. This is not a clue I'm excited to follow. Not if it means what I think it does, anyway. "You don't think they expect us to make a trapeze out of this, do you?"

West flashes his light up to the ceiling. He starts on one end and slowly uses a crisscross pattern until he gets to the center, where his light suddenly stops. "Uh-oh."

I don't like that tone. The last time I heard it, we were nowhere near beating a room at Escape City, and West announced that we had less than five minutes before the buzzer.

Angling my flashlight upward, I add my beam to his. There, sticking out from the ceiling, is a large metal hook.

I let out a strangled gasp. "No. No way."

"They want us to hook this rope on there and do what? Swing around?" Hannah says with a half laugh. "That seems a little dangerous, and if *I'm* saying that..."

Hannah doesn't have to finish her sentence for us to get her drift. Hannah loves adventure and rarely gets nervous. If she thinks something looks dangerous, it most definitely is.

"This was built a long time ago, guys. I don't think they were as worried about people getting hurt and suing them." West sighs. "Plus, the funhouse never opened. They probably planned to put a net up or something and never had the chance."

I'm so nervous I'm shaking. From the moment we saw that hook, my brain started calculating risk. And swinging from a ceiling this high is ridiculously risky. No net. No padded flooring. Just a wood floor to break your fall.

The circus theme has officially gone too far.

"I guess the stairwell makes sense now," Hannah says gravely. "It's not even real, just a ledge to jump off of."

My stomach lurches. "What would we even be swinging to? There isn't another platform on the other side of the room."

"Let's go up the stairs," West suggests. "I'm guessing we'll find some answers up there."

Yeah, scary answers. Answers about swinging around like monkeys with no harnesses or safety nets.

I move to follow him, but he puts out a hand to stop me. "I can go first. Just wait here."

Embarrassment heats my cheeks. "No. No one goes anywhere alone in here, remember? That's the rule. We all go or none of us go."

West lifts his chin and turns on his heel. Hannah and I follow him in single file up the narrow staircase. As the ground gets more and more distant, the knots in my stomach tighten.

Stopping at the top, West pops the end of his flashlight into his mouth so his hands are free. He grips the railing and pulls off a long metal pole.

I drag the rest of the rope up behind me and laugh weakly. "What is that?"

He turns it over in his hands. There's a hook on one end. Tugging on it, the pole extends. "I think we're supposed to use this to hang the rope on that hook. It's too far away from here to reach."

"O-kay, but what then?" My eyes glide down to the

ground below, and I grip the railing tighter. "There's no platform. Even after we hook that rope to the hook in the ceiling, there's nothing to swing to. We'd just hit a wall!"

West thinks for a second, then says. "Hold up. Maybe not. Hear me out. The walls in this room aren't all solid, right? We know there are passages hidden in them because we found one. *Annnnd* the third exit that will let us into the next room is still hidden somewhere! Maybe we couldn't find it before because it isn't down there." He gestures at the ground.

Oh. Maybe the third hidden exit is up here.

I shine my flashlight from the hook in the ceiling to the wall on the other side of the room. Sure enough, the wallpaper there looks strange, like the stripes don't quite line up the way they should. I crack my knuckles, sensing a challenge. Too bad it's a challenge I would normally run from.

"West is right. We won't hit a wall. We'll hit the third hidden door." I run my light around the outline in a square so West and Hannah can see what I'm talking about. "This rope is the only way to get to it."

"So, the triplets expect us to swing over and just crash into it?" West asks incredulously.

Hannah flashes a mischievous smile. It's the same smile I saw when she convinced me that toilet papering the tree in our evil math teacher's front yard was a good idea.

Spoiler alert: it wasn't. It didn't *seem* risky, but that's because I didn't realize that Mr. Tersing has a camera installed on his front porch. I ended up grounded for a week.

"Fortune favors the bold, remember?" Hannah finally says. "They chose those words for a reason. It has to be our motto in here. If we want to find the treasure, anyway."

Her words echo through the cavernous space, sending shivers up my spine. What are the odds that we could get hurt doing this? Pretty good. The rope is old. There's a chance it could break or slip off the hook. The door hidden in the wall is just a theory. There's a chance we could swing over to it and knock ourselves unconscious. Then there's the worst chance of all...the chance I panic and fall.

I look up to realize both West and Hannah are staring at me.

"It's risky," I admit. "But if our theory about the rule of threes is solid, I think this is the only route left."

West meets my eyes. He's the only one who knows about my secret fear of heights. I don't hide it, really; I just don't put myself in situations where heights are going to be a thing. "What do you want to do?" he asks quietly.

I want to make it through this funhouse and find the treasure. I want to save my parents' house, to save *us* from drowning in the stacks of bills piled up on her desk. I want

Mom to be able to sleep again and Dad to have a nurse more often. I want us to be a family again, a happy family that gets to watch movies together and isn't so stressed all the time.

I look from the rope in my hands to the hook in the ceiling, and then over to the spot where we *think* the door is. Even though every cell in my body is screaming *no*, I squeeze past Hannah and take up a spot next to West on the landing.

"I want to go first."

CHAPTER TEN

THE DARING YOUNG GIRL
ON THE FLYING TRAPEZE

West's tongue has been out of his mouth so long I'm afraid it's going to dry out and turn into a crunchy pink potato chip.

"Al-most there," he grunts, maneuvering the pole and the rope closer to the hook in the ceiling. "You good, Hannah?"

"Mmm-hmm," she answers, clearly focused on her job. We decided that since the pole is heavy and awkward once it's extended, she would hold the back end to share some of the weight. All those years of holding positions in ballet must've given her great endurance, because she seems like she could do this forever. Meanwhile, a drop of sweat is running down West's temple, and his face is the color of a fire truck.

When the clip finally slides into place, we all breathe a sigh of relief.

Well, sort of. There can't be *that* much relief when you know what you have to do next and it's terrifying.

"Ugh," Hannah sets down the back end of the pole and shakes her arms out. "That was uncomfortable."

"No kidding," West says. He slowly begins retracting the pole, careful not to let go of the rope. As it draws closer and closer, my heart beats faster and faster. By the time he has the end of the rope in his hands, I feel like I'm having a heart attack.

"You're sure about this?" he asks me. There's a glimmer of something in his eyes. Concern, I think. West is a lot like me. Careful. Practical. *Not* adventurous. If anyone should be jonesing to swing across this room, it should be Hannah. She's the brave one.

Still, I step forward.

"I'm sure. I'm the one who needs the treasure. I'm the one who dragged us here. This was all my idea." I reach out and take the rope from him, then step toward the edge of the platform. The ground looks so far away from up here. At least thirty feet by my calculations.

Thirty feet would be a bad fall.

The rope is prickly and heavy in my hands. It feels like a warning.

Mess this up, and the treasure isn't all you'll lose.

Fear spikes through my veins. I can do this. I'm not Hannah, who would probably leap off this ledge without even thinking about it, but I'm also not a chicken. I'm here... I'm fighting for my family. I'm also fighting for the Deltas. If I move away, what will become of us? Sure, we can call and text and FaceTime but it's not the same. West and Hannah are the best thing that ever happened to me. I can't lose them.

"I hope they measured this rope correctly," I say, gripping it tighter. This is the side of my brain that never turns off. The *what if* side. "What if this is the wrong length and I swing over and smack into the wrong section of the wall?"

"I'm pretty sure they measured it. Look," West points at a spot just above where I'm gripping. A thick black piece of tape is wrapped around the rope. Drawn on the tape, an image. This time, it's a compass. The third symbol!

"He's right. I think you're supposed to hold on to the rope there," Hannah says. "You sure you don't want me to do this? Honestly, it looks really fun."

Right. Fun. I shake my head, hoping I look more confident than I feel. Then I slide my palms up the rope until the black line is hidden underneath. "I'm good. Once I'm on the other side, I'll toss the rope back to you guys. Just be ready to catch it."

Hannah playfully nudges West to the side. "I got this. I've seen you catch a basketball in gym. It's not pretty."

West's mouth flops open. "Jeez, Hannah."

"Sorry! I just meant that you say the exact same thing every time we're in a new escape room, and I think we should take your advice right now."

A puzzled expression takes over his face. "I have never told you that you can't catch."

Hannah laughs. "No! Not that. I mean that you always say we need to know and use our talents." She shoos at him like he's a fly buzzing around her lunch. "Your talent just isn't catching."

Despite my nerves, a laugh bubbles out of me. West takes a step down to make more room on the ledge for Hannah and me.

I inch to the edge until my toes are hanging off. My whole body is shaking, and my brain is screaming at me to stop, to take the time to figure out some calculations before I do this.

How long is the rope?

How far is the drop?

Are we sure the door is there and I'm not going to flatten myself?

For once, I don't have the answers. All I can do is believe

that if I do my best, everything will be okay. That's what Dad always says anyway. Then again, he always did his best, and it still didn't stop the CFS from getting him.

Don't worry, Dad. I'm going to get us out of this mess.

With a final steadying breath, I take a step back. Then another. When my back touches the railing and I have nowhere else to go, I run at the edge...and jump. My stomach immediately bottoms out like on the big drop on a roller coaster. I grit my teeth and fight the scream building in my throat. Everything goes by so fast, nothing but a blur of darkness, flashlight beams, and red and white stripes. It all happens so quickly I barely have enough time to squeeze my eyes shut before I'm at the wall.

There's a loud tearing sound as I break through. I hit the floor in a heap of something cold and crinkly. Like a shower curtain or sheet of plastic. Whatever it is, it's covering my face so I can't see my surroundings. The only thing I can tell is that it's dark. Dark and musty. I continue to grip the rope tightly, afraid of accidentally letting it go.

"Sarah? Sarah!"

West's voice snaps me out of my haze. I tug the plastic off my head and stand up. "I'm here! I'm okay."

Looking across the room at West and Hannah on the ledge, the fear I felt moments before melts away. I did it. I conquered my fear of heights. I made it through the hidden door without dying!

"Well?" Hannah yells, dropping her hands to her hips. "What's it like over there?"

I look behind me but can't see much. I'm not even sure if the room I'm in is big or small. One thing I am sure of, though, is that we are the first people to enter it. The fact that the door was still covered in plastic proves it.

"Can't tell. I stuck my flashlight back in West's backpack before I came over here." I hold the rope up and wait for Hannah's signal before launching it back in her direction. She catches it easily. "Who is coming over next?"

Hannah looks at West. They talk, but it's too quiet for me to make out what they're saying from across the room. Then West steps up and takes the rope from Hannah's hands.

"I'm coming over next," he shouts.

I fight a smirk. "Is it because Hannah doesn't think you'll be able to catch the rope if she comes over next?"

"No!" he barks, then rolls his eyes. "All right, yes. Whatever. Just be ready to catch me if I can't stop myself."

Catch him? Has West seen himself lately? Unlike most seventh-grade guys at our school, he's not all skinny arms and legs. He's bigger. Catching him is going to be as easy as catching a piano.

West grips the rope and looks down at the ground nervously. "Do you think I'm too heavy for this? I'm a lot bigger than you, and I've got the backpack too."

How do I answer that? There's no way to know if the triplets even thought about weight limits in the fifties. "Give Hannah the backpack if that makes you feel better, but I'm sure they planned for adults to go through here, and you're about the size of an adult, so it's fine."

A wave of nerves hits me as he hands off the backpack and shuffles backward, preparing to jump. As scared as I was to swing across, I'm almost more scared now that West and Hannah are going to do it. I don't know what I'd do if one of them got hurt. Never forgive myself, that's for sure.

"Ready?" he asks, making eye contact with me.

"Ready." I stand back, away from the opening, and hold my arms out.

Without missing a beat, he whooshes forward and makes the jump. He drops briefly; then the rope tightens and West swings in my direction. I notice his eyes are clenched shut and his feet are wrapped around the rope.

Wait.

His feet are wrapped around the rope.

That means he won't be able to...

West crashes into me before I can even finish my thought.

I grip him as tightly as I can, panicking when his body weight begins pulling us back toward the edge.

"West, put your feet down!" I scream. "Now!"

He does more than put down his feet. He lets go of the rope and falls in a heap onto the floor. I fall with him. The rope slips away from both of us, the end writhing across the floor and toward the edge like a snake.

"No!" I shriek, clamoring after it on my hands and knees. Catching the knotted end, I exhale and flop onto my back. Dust billows up around me, making us both cough.

"Guys?" Hannah yells. "What is going on over there?"

I sit up and look at West, who looks more dazed than the time he came home from the dentist after having a bad cavity filled. "We're fine. Everything is fine. West is never going to be Tarzan, that's all."

"Can't catch and can't swing," Hannah answers with a cackle. "Good thing you have that great memory going for you, buddy."

"Ha, ha," he finally answers, brushing the dust out of his hair and off his pants. "You can't talk yet. You haven't done it."

"Oh. Yeah? Watch me." Hannah lifts the rope I just threw back to her in the air with a wicked smile. She lets out a bellow and leaps. Time stops as I watch my fearless friend glide through the air. Like everything else she does, she's graceful. No fear. No panic on her face. Just sheer joy. You'd think she was on a ride at Walt Disney World instead of risking her life on a makeshift trapeze.

West and I move out of the way so she has enough room to swing through the opening in the wall. We don't even need to catch her. She lets go and lands on her feet like the whole thing was rehearsed.

"Show-off," West mutters.

Hannah takes a dramatic bow.

For a moment the feeling is back. That wild, proud rush of adrenaline from the Deltas standing in a room no one has been in. Not since the fifties! The feeling is quickly replaced with a sinking feeling when I realize none of us are holding on to the rope.

I walk back to the edge, scowling. The rope is swaying gently in the middle of the room again. "Oh no. I *really* hope we didn't need that."

"Doesn't matter. Even if Hannah had held on to it, we couldn't have gotten it unhooked from the ceiling without the pole," West says. "And the pole is still on the other side."

"The rope was heavy too," Hannah adds. "No way it would fit in this backpack, and we wouldn't be able to carry it through the rest of this place."

I swallow through the thickness in my throat and sneak a glance at my cell phone. Still no signal.

"I know we couldn't take the rope with us, but we should have attached it over here somehow. What if something happens, and our only choice is to come back this way later? Without a rope on this side, we won't be able to get down to the first floor where the exit is." I creep to the edge and look down. "It's way too high."

West and Hannah exchange an alarmed look.

"I really hope that doesn't happen, but if it does," West says, "we'd be stuck."

Exactly. And even worse than being stuck?

No one knows where we are.

CHAPTER ELEVEN
THE BOX ROOM

"Wow," West says. He's looking up at the ceiling of the new room, mesmerized.

"Flashlight?" I ask, holding my hand out. West takes his bag back from Hannah and fishes one out for me.

I shine the light up and move it around. Dozens and dozens of colorful wooden boxes are dangling from hooks connected to a metal track in the ceiling. They're close enough to reach up and touch, but none of us dare to. Not yet.

"Too bad this place isn't like that temple in the movie you were talking about earlier." Hannah says, squinting. "It would be awesome to find a lit torch on a wall. Anything to help us see a little better."

West extends his hand to Hannah. "Give me the

backpack. I have something that might help us. I went through our camping supplies before we left and found a couple small lanterns."

"Since when do you go camping?" I ask incredulously. I can see West doing a lot of things with his family. Alphabetizing bookshelves. Color-coding the kitchen cabinets. Memorizing the periodic table. But camping? No way. West isn't exactly outdoorsy.

"I go camping!" he insists. "Okay, I went once. But I was in charge of keeping all of our supplies organized."

Hannah snorts. "Of course, you were."

He shoots her a dark look as he unzips the pack. "Shut up. Bug spray and bandages are no good to anyone unless you can find them!"

Hannah and I laugh.

"Hey, it's too dark in here," West says, fighting a smile of his own. "Someone shine a flashlight in the bag so that I can see."

I do as he asks, feeling optimistic when he pulls two collapsible lanterns out. Those are going to be useful.

West turns them both on and sets them on opposite sides of the room. They're brighter than I expected them to be. Without all the shadows, the room isn't nearly as spooky. It's not decorated in the same circus theme as downstairs, but instead looks rustic. Like a cabin. Wood walls, a fireplace in the corner, and even some very old and dusty taxidermy animal heads hanging. There are some copper pots dangling on hooks above the fireplace, and inside, a fake fire made from colored cardboard. Interesting. Just like the last room was supposed to make us feel like we were inside a real circus tent, this room actually reminds me of a cozy lake house.

I do a double take at the nearest taxidermy head. It isn't just any old taxidermy, like a deer or something; it's a... goat? "That's weird."

"No kidding. Who hangs a goat in their funhouse?" Hannah asks, her face pinched.

"The same kind of person who hangs a peacock," West says, pointing to the colorful bird in the corner. Besides the boxes hanging down from the ceiling, it's the only color in the room. It's also big and just a teeny-tiny bit scary. I make the decision that I don't want to meet a peacock in real life.

I stand on my tiptoes so I can look the goat in its eyes. They're dull, probably from so many years of neglect. "I don't know if these heads are even real. They look fake, don't they?"

West rolls his shoulders. "I don't know. I'm more

83

worried about this." He taps on the only door in the room. At least the only one we can see. There can always be more hidden in the floor or the walls. As long as there aren't any we have to swing through, I'll be okay.

"Locked?" Hannah asks.

He jiggles the doorknob. "Yup. But glad we checked. It would be embarrassing to spend a bunch of time in here looking for a key we don't even need."

I imagine a checklist in my mind. We've found one door. *Check.* No keys though. "We should still keep our eyes open for different exits. Hidden ones."

I tap on the wall. It sounds solid. "There were three different exits in the circus room. I'm guessing they all led to different parts of the house."

"Like one of those choose-your-own-adventure books," West says. "I loved those things when I was little. You could pick what you wanted the character to do, and there were a bunch of different outcomes, so technically you could read the book more than once, and it would always be different."

"Bet that's what the triplets were doing with this house too," I say. "If they wanted people to come back more than once, they had to make it so that they didn't experience the exact same thing again."

"So the trapeze door led us here, but what about the other doors?" Hannah asks.

I shrug. "We won't know where those doors lead unless we come across another room where it's clear someone else has been in there."

The idea of a choose-your-own-adventure funhouse is cool, but unsettling. It's exciting to be in a room that no one else has been in, but that doesn't mean that someone else hasn't gotten farther in this house than us. We just aren't on the same path they took. And if someone else *did* get farther, they could have found the treasure.

"Maybe the key to the next room is in one of these," Hannah suggests, swatting at one of the boxes overhead.

"Could be. I mean, there's definitely *something* hidden in them," I say. "The question is, what is it and which box is it in?" I head to the other side of the room, yelping when I smack into something that stops me in my tracks.

West and Hannah are at my side instantly. I rub at my sore forehead, confused. "What just happened?"

Putting a palm out in front of her, Hannah gasps. "It's like a giant window. The room is divided in half by glass!"

Yikes. I've seen videos of people running into sliding doors and stuff because the glass was so clean, but it's not nearly as funny when it happens to you.

"Guess that means we can only open the boxes on this side of the room for now. I don't see a way over to that side," West says, shining his flashlight up to where the glass meets the ceiling and then down to the floor.

"Hey," Hannah says, shining her flashlight on the bottom of a box. "The boxes all have symbols on them!"

I do the same, narrowing my eyes on the small image etched into the bottom of each one. It's the same three symbols we saw in the circus room: the wishbone, the deck of cards, and the compass.

"Looks like we need to figure out what those mean now. They could be our clue to which box we're supposed to choose." I glance at West, who is still examining the boxes and looking extra froggy while doing it.

"We should open a box with the wishbone on it for sure," Hannah announces. "If it means luck, then that seems smart, right?"

I shake my head. "I don't know. Could be too easy."

"If the wishbone stands for luck, maybe the compass stands for something with directions or navigating." West lowers his flashlight. "Like maybe that symbol will help us with routes or secret passages—if there are any."

"Ooh, like their version of a map! How to get from point A to point B," Hannah adds.

An idea jolts me. "There was a compass on the rope, remember? I bet that was to help people figure out that the rope was supposed to be used to get into the next room."

West groans. "All of this makes sense, but it isn't really helping. I still don't know which box we should open. The symbols all seem like they *could* work."

We sit in silence for a moment. Despite not being very big, the room is drafty, and the boxes sway gently above us.

"We're wasting time," Hannah says. Before either of us can stop her, she reaches up and plucks down the first box in the row.

I stare at it in horror. Even though we might have ended up guessing anyway, I still thought we'd at least pick one of the three symbols first. Hannah just isn't patient. She never has been.

West runs a hand through his hair. His eyes are wide, and his mouth open in an *O* shape. "I cannot believe you just did that without talking to us."

"Well, we don't exactly have time to take a vote on it, West. Seriously. Besides, nothing bad happened. For all we know, there's a key in here!" With this, she cracks open the lid. A soft tinkling sound drifts out. It reminds me of a music box. Except, there's a rolled slip of paper spinning where the plastic ballerina should be.

Hannah removes the paper, then sets the box on the floor so she can unravel it. It's wrapped up like a scroll. "*Beware of wrong choices; for those you shall pay. Be wise and choose carefully; strategy saves the day.*"

Suddenly, there's a foreign sound on the other side of the room. A box falls from the ceiling and breaks open as it hits the floor. Wood pieces scatter everywhere. Unlike Hannah's box, it looks empty. No key, no paper, nothing.

"What the...?" I say, rushing over to the glass to get a better look. "So picking a box from this side makes a box fall on *that side*?"

"Looks like it. We should've known this was harder than it looked," West says. "The box with the key in it will probably be on that side of the glass. Even if we manage to make it to fall, then we'll have to figure out how to get to it."

My stomach sinks. "Ugh. This is bad. If the triplets used the rule of threes in here too, then that means we might only have two choices left." I pace in a tight circle. "And the riddle is pretty clear; mistakes are going to cost us."

Hannah's face crumbles. "Do you think I just screwed this up?"

I want to put my arm around her, tell her it's okay, but something stops me. Maybe it's that what just happened is just so *Hannah*. She's impulsive and has set us back in more than one escape room because of it. And if anyone stands to lose today from her making quick, silly decisions, it's me.

"Maybe," I tell her, deciding not to sugarcoat the truth. "You've gotta stop doing stuff like that. We're *a team*. We're supposed to make decisions as a team!"

I'm aware of my voice getting louder, but I can't help it. Hannah knows how important this treasure is to me.

A lone tear rolls down her cheek. "I'm sorry. I know we're a team. I just…I just want to be helpful."

Despite my frustration, seeing her cry is upsetting. "Then don't do anything unless we all agree on it, okay?"

Out of the corner of my eye, I see West's face. He looks unsettled.

"What?" I ask him, feeling ruffled. "You're acting like you don't agree, but I know you do. You plan more than Hannah and me combined!"

"No, you're right. I agree," he starts. "Hannah shouldn't have done that, but we're still okay. We have two more guesses, and I'm pretty sure that this"—he takes the scroll from Hannah and holds it up—"was a clue. *Strategy*."

I look back at the spot where Hannah pulled the box from. It was the first box in the line. No wonder it had the clue about strategy in it. Most people would probably grab that one first, but that's definitely not strategic.

"O-kay, so we know we need to be strategic about which boxes to pick. But how?" My eyes glide over the rows and rows of boxes. "There are at least fifty boxes here, half on one side and half on the other. That means we have a very low chance of picking the right box unless we can narrow this down."

"Let's narrow it then," West says. He sounds more confident now. "What symbol is on the bottom of that box, Hannah?"

She lifts it up and turns it over. "A compass."

"Then let's not choose any more boxes with a compass on them. And let's not choose the wishbone. It was a big clue in the first room, but they already told us there's more to this room than luck. That just leaves—"

"The deck of cards," I finish for him. "That has to be it! Before my dad got sick, he used to have buddies over once a month to play cards. Blackjack. There's a ton of strategy in that game!"

"Exactly!" West says. He shines his flashlight back up again, bouncing from box to box. His lips are moving as he counts. "There are sixty boxes. Fifty-nine if we take out the one Hannah chose and the one that fell. That means if there are equal numbers of each symbol, then there should be twenty boxes with the deck of cards on them."

My brain starts twitching with numbers. If there are only twenty boxes with the deck of cards on them total, then that means there are only ten on our side of the glass. It also means with only ten boxes to choose from, our odds just got much, much better.

"I can't believe I'm saying this, but we might have to guess a second time." West says. "There are ten unopened boxes on this side that could work. Maybe we pull down one more and see if there's a new clue in it or if anything different happens?"

"I hate guessing," I tell him.

"I know, but I'd rather make another mistake than waste more time. You?"

I don't know how to answer his question. All I know is that picking another box randomly makes me feel like I'm going to puke. If it's the wrong one again, we might only have one more chance.

Hannah sniffles. I realize now that she's standing behind us and hasn't said a thing. I lean over and playfully bump into her. "I'm sorry I yelled at you."

"I'm sorry I was stupid," she answers. "I know how important this is."

The sadness in her voice makes me feel bad. "It wasn't stupid. It was just...overconfident. But we're okay now. It's going to be okay."

West reaches up and touches the box directly above him.

It has a clear deck of cards printed on the bottom. "Deltas? We need to make a decision, like yesterday. Should I pull it down, or no?"

Hannah reaches out and grabs my hand. Her eyes are soft, apologetic. I nod at her, and she nods back before saying to West, "Do it."

CHAPTER TWELVE
THE TRUTH

With a sharp tug, West pulls the box off the string. His eyebrows knit together as he opens it and looks inside.

"Is there another clue?" Hannah asks.

"Or a key?" I add, even though I know the odds are bad. The triplets almost definitely put the key on the other side of the glass. They wanted this to be as challenging—scratch that—as *frustrating* as possible.

He turns the box over and over in his hands. "It has another rolled-up paper in it."

Taking the paper out, he unfurls it and begins to read.

"*In threes it has been, and threes it shall be,*" he reads aloud, "*but know there is more to this room than you see.*"

Just like before, a box falls on the other side of the room

and breaks open. We run to the glass, groaning when we see it's empty as well.

"Well, the riddle is proof that they're using the rule of threes. Don't know what the end of that means though. More to this room than we see?" Hannah says.

"It's kind of like the phrase, 'More than meets the eye,'" West says. "Could mean the same thing, I guess." He scratches his head and stares longingly at the wooden boxes on the other side of the glass.

The riddle doesn't surprise me. There's always more to escape rooms than it seems. A really good one looks simple at first. It's not until you've been sweating, running, and digging around in it for twenty minutes that you realize how confusing it actually is.

"Wait." I look back up at the boxes, realizing we're doing this backward. "We should have picked the box we want to fall first. If we can figure out which box on that side of the room has the key in it, maybe we can figure out how to make that specific one fall."

West claps loudly. "Yes. *Yesssss*! The triplets want us to use strategy in here, which means there must be a pattern."

Hannah's face and palms are pressed against the glass. Suddenly she spins around, her face flushed and excited. "I think I see a box over there that's different!"

West and I rush to her side. Hannah is using her pointer finger to count the boxes.

"Second row, third box from our right," she says. "It's a different shape, right? Not really a rectangle like the others?"

I clap a hand over my mouth, excited. She's right. The box has a pointed top that widens into four corners at the bottom.

"It's a triangle-shaped box," West says, grinning. "More triangles. Anyone else starting to think this is a little creepy? Like the triplets created this funhouse for us?"

"I thought that before! It is *really* coincidental. Maybe they were more like us than we know. Nerdy numbers people." I elbow West teasingly, then do the same to Hannah.

"Hey!" she barks with a laugh. "Speak for yourself! I am not nerdy."

West smirks. "Oh, you're *very* nerdy. You just don't want to admit it yet. Don't worry, before you know it, you'll be organizing camping supplies for fun too."

Hannah cringes, but the smile on her face is impossible to miss.

This is how it always is with us. We might not fit in with everyone else, but we fit perfectly together.

I tap on the glass. "So, if the box Hannah noticed is the one with the key in it, we need to calculate which box to pull down on our side to make it fall."

"Right. Seems simple to me. If pulling this one down"—West touches the empty string—"made that box fall, then if we pull a box three spots away, that *should* make a box three spots away from the empty string over there fall. Right?"

My head is spinning with this possible pattern. It makes sense, but funhouses aren't supposed to make sense. There could still be a trick here somewhere. And our next guess could be our last one.

That's a lot of pressure.

"Wait. I get what you're saying, but there's still a choice here. You could pull a box three spots this way"—I gesture down the row of boxes toward the stuffed goat—"or three spots that way back toward the door we came through."

"There's no way to narrow down the pattern unless we try one of them." West points to two different boxes. Both have the deck of cards symbol etched into the bottom. "One of these *should* make the triangular box fall. The other one will..." He trails off, a concerned expression taking over his tired face.

The other one will do *something*. Hopefully that something isn't bad.

"We have a fifty-fifty chance of choosing the correct one," I say, just in case anyone is fuzzy on our odds at the moment.

"Fifty-fifty isn't bad. I say pull down that one," Hannah suggests. "It has the most green on it, and that's my favorite color."

"I thought blue was your favorite color," I say.

"It was," she answers. "Last week. This week it's green."

I'd laugh if I wasn't so nervous. Only Hannah would have a different favorite color every week. "All right then. Go for it. C'mon green!"

West's jaw clenches as he yanks the box down. He opens it slowly, his expression a mix of anticipation and fear. I know what's inside before he even holds it up. The frown on his face is a dead giveaway.

Another rolled-up paper and another riddle.

> *Bravely you tried, but sadly you failed.*
> *Another chance you will get; your ship has not*
> *sailed! Find the right box, and then you may*
> *see, the path is quite clear to reaching the key.*

Just like before, a box falls on the other side of the glass. I sigh, telling myself that even though we chose wrong, at least we know the pattern now. All we need to do is pick the other box next—the one three spots away in the opposite direction.

Before we can even decode the new riddle, something happens. There's a mechanical sound, like something being cranked or turned. The remaining boxes judder and sway as if they're about to move.

Then they do.

On both sides of the glass, the metal rail attached to the ceiling lurches with a groan. The boxes slowly travel until they're in totally different spots. It reminds me of the times I've gone with Mom to pick up clothes at the dry cleaners. The clothes are covered in plastic and hung on a moving track. All the person has to do is push a button, and the track rotates so they can easily find what they're looking for. Only in this case, the triplets are moving the boxes so we *can't* find what we're looking for. I imagine them watching us and feeling pleased with themselves, my teeth clenching together.

There really was more to this room than we could see.

Hannah drops her head into her hands and whimpers.

West rubs at his eyes, looking wearier by the minute. "The boxes are attached to a conveyor belt. I can't believe we didn't notice that before. It must reset their positions after three wrong choices."

"I'm so sorry, guys. If I hadn't snatched that first box down so fast, this would never have happened." Hannah brushes a fresh round of tears away. "I don't know why I do stuff like that. I guess I always feel like I'm the weakest one here. Like I don't figure stuff out as fast or as well as you guys do."

I wrap an arm around her and squeeze. "It would have happened no matter what. This is a hard challenge, and I don't think there is any way to complete it without guessing, at least at first." I hug Hannah tighter as her shoulders begin to shake. "You aren't weak, Hannah."

Her watery eyes meet mine. They're sad. Really, *really* sad. "I am though. There's something I need to tell you guys."

West stops checking the bottom of the newly reset boxes and blinks at her. "That sounds serious."

"It is." She takes a deep, shaky breath. "And I should have told you before. Remember when I told you that I quit dance? I didn't."

I blink at her, confused.

"How is that possible?" West asks. "You have tons of time to hang out with us lately, and you never did when you were dancing. Your schedule was insane."

"Yeah. I'm not dancing. I didn't *quit* though," she clarifies. "I failed out. Everyone else got their pointe shoes but me. I just wasn't good enough, I guess."

I'm so surprised I can hardly speak. Hannah was always so dedicated to ballet. Never missed a class, never skipped a workout. West and I thought it was weird that she quit out of nowhere, but it's even weirder to think she failed...and hid it from us.

"Why?" I ask quietly. "Why didn't you tell us? We could have helped you through all that."

"I was embarrassed. I didn't want anyone to know, even you guys." She sniffles into her arm. "Ever since then, I try so hard at everything. I don't want to feel like that ever again. Like a big loser."

"You could never be a loser, Hannah," West says. His voice is soft and kind. "You're a Delta." He wraps his arm around her too, placing Hannah between us.

"Failing out of dance sucked, but letting you guys down would be so much worse. I think that's why I make decisions so fast. I keep hoping someday my choice will be the right one, and I'll save the day, you know? I'll be the one who finds the key or the hidden door or the treasure."

My heart breaks for her. My friend who always seems cheerful, always seems like the world is her oyster, she's just as unsure of herself as the rest of us. I just didn't notice it.

"You're the one who told me about this place, remember? Without you, we wouldn't even be here," I remind her. "You're also the one who hummed songs for us to guess the whole train ride here so we wouldn't get bored, and brought everyone gum, and swung across the Circus Room with the backpack like it was nothing. You do a lot, Hannah. You just don't give yourself any credit."

Hannah dries her tears with the back of her sleeve. "You really liked my humming?"

West and I burst into laughter.

"We loved it," I answer, wrapping her in a bear hug. "You're like our personal hype squad. Without you, West and I would be so anxious we'd probably murder each other!"

Swiping at her face one final time, Hannah straightens and lifts her chin. "All right then. Time to slay this room. We have three brand-new chances to get. That. Key!"

Her face still damp with tears, Hannah holds her hands up in the triangle symbol. West and I do the same. I hate failing more than I hate guessing, but really, this room wasn't a total failure. In fact, it might've been one of the best rooms we've ever done, and that's saying something since we don't even have the key yet.

We still have something pretty great though.

Each other.

CHAPTER THIRTEEN
A GOAT WEARING LIPSTICK

"Finally," West says, swiping his hair away from his eyes. "I was afraid we'd never get the right box to fall."

I press my palms to the glass divider and look at the new box that has fallen. Like the others, it split into two pieces when it hit the ground. The lid is lying upside down and the bottom half is on its side about a foot away. Then there's the exciting part, the thing that made us all scream when it tumbled out. *The key.* I stare at it, annoyed that it's within reach, but we can't touch it.

Hannah is pacing up and down the glass barrier. "There has to be a way over there. Maybe we need to go back into to the Circus Room."

West raises an eyebrow skeptically. "We can't. No rope,

remember? Besides, we've only done two escape rooms where we had to go backward for something. Once we get into a new room or space, we usually find clues that will keep us moving *forward* in there."

I nod. West would know. He can probably remember every single escape room we've ever done and where the clues were. If he says we don't usually go backward, I believe him.

Reaching out, I take the strange riddle about ships from West's hand and reread it.

Bravely you tried, but sadly you failed. Another chance you will get; your ship has not sailed! Find the right box, and then you may see, the path is quite clear to reaching the key.

"The path is *not* clear," West complains. Despite the chill in the room, his cheeks are stained pink. "There's a giant glass wall between us and that stupid key!"

"Maybe that riddle isn't talking about the glass. Maybe it's talking about the other door you found, West. The locked one. There could be another key hidden in this room," Hannah says. "A key that will open the locked door and"—she gestures wildly—"*finally* get us to the other side of the room."

"I like this theory. That door"—West points at the door he found when we first got into this room—"*might* lead to the other side. It could easily open into a hallway that connects the two entrances in this room. See the door over there?"

I look through the glass. The other side of the room has more strange taxidermy animals, wooden walls, pots on the wall, and...a door. The knob is wooden, just like the walls, and engraved with the deck of cards symbol.

"Strategy," I say for what feels like the hundredth time. "If there was a strategy to finding the key, then there has to be a strategy to getting to it."

We look around the room in silence. There are moments like this in every escape room, seconds or even minutes when you think you're failing. When there are no obvious answers. We always get past them, though. Sometimes it's easier than others, but the Deltas never give up.

One of our lanterns flickers. Hannah gasps. "Oh jeez. If we end up in the dark in this place, I'm not going to be happy."

West laughs. "Don't tell me you're afraid of the dark, Hannah."

"You're not?" She asks with a dramatic shudder. "I don't care what anyone says. The dark is scary. It's easier for things to hide in the dark."

It's easier for things to hide in the dark.

I roll the thought over and over in my mind. "Hannah! That's it! Guys, turn off the lanterns!"

"What? No!" Hannah whines. "I just admitted I hate the dark. Is this payback?"

"Payback for what?" I ask.

"For the fact that I told you about the broccoli stuck in your teeth the other day?"

I laugh unexpectedly. "Um, no. I was happy you told me about the broccoli, you weirdo. I need the lights off because I want to use the UV light again to see if there are any clues in here."

Without hesitation, West flicks off the first lantern, then the other. Hannah huddles by my side as I turn on the UV light and begin running it over the walls. At first, I don't see anything but more random splotches and stains. Then I get to the stuffed goat head. The fur and eyes look normal. But the mouth...the mouth is glowing!

"Look!" I say, leaning closer to the goat. "Do you guys see that?"

West nods excitedly. "Looks like it's wearing lipstick. That's gotta be a clue, right? A lipstick-wearing goat?"

A snort bubbles out of Hannah. "Seems like a possibility. We had to become trapeze artists to get into this room. Looks like we need to dig around in a goat mouth to get into the next one."

"I seriously can't believe I'm about to do this," West says, eyeing the goat carefully for a moment before sticking a finger in the small gap between its lips.

"Anything?" I ask.

He sticks a second finger in, then wiggles it around, grunting. "Yeah. Yeah, there's definitely something in here!"

"Probably a tarantula," Hannah says with a dark chuckle.

I elbow her, laughing at the *oomph* sound she makes.

West finally pulls his fingers out of the goat's mouth, revealing a silver key. "Jackpot!"

"A key so we can get to the other key." I turn the UV light off and my normal flashlight on. "The triplets really were weird."

Hannah snatches the key from West's palm and immediately races to the door. Jamming it in the lock, she flings the door open. Then we all stare, wide-eyed and open-mouthed at what's on the other side. Not a hallway. Not a tunnel.

A wall.

The door opens to a brick wall.

I slap my hand against my forehead. "You have got to be kidding me."

Hannah presses on the bricks. When they don't revolve, shift, or do anything interesting, she kicks at them with an annoyed grunt.

"So I stuck my hand in that stupid goat mouth for nothing," West says, clearly frustrated. "*And* we're back at square one. No way to get to the other side of the room."

Even in the darkness, I can see that Hannah's forehead is bunched up with lines.

"What are you thinking?" I ask.

"I'm thinking we have to go through this somehow." She walks back to the center of the room and taps on the glass. "We're losing too much time in here. Maybe we just break it?"

I imagine how fun it would be to shatter the glass. Maybe we could even use the goat head to do it.

"We probably could, but I don't think that's the answer," West says, interrupting my fantasy. "If the triplets expected people to break this, then how would they reset the room for other people to go through it? They couldn't have replaced the glass every time."

West is right. That would've too hard and too expensive for the triplets to manage.

I run a palm over the glass, baffled. We're missing something. We have to be.

Shining my flashlight over the glass, I frown at my reflection. Dirt smudged on my cheek, probably from the floor of the Circus Room. Frizzy hair. Wild, confused eyes. And that line on my forehead.

Wait.

Line on my forehead?

I lean in, realizing the line isn't on my forehead, but on the glass itself. It's so thin that it's virtually invisible. My eyes follow it up to the ceiling, then back down to the floor. Sure, it could just be a seam or an imperfection in the glass, but what if it's not? What if it's another one of the triplets' tricks?

No, not a trick. A strategy. Hide the door in plain sight. Of course! Escape rooms do it all the time. The most obvious door is a fake clue, or a *red herring* as mystery books and movies would call it. Only difference is that if the triplets' funhouse had actually opened, there would be electricity in the building, and this room would have been well lit. It probably would have taken us half the time if it wasn't so dim in here. *Blah.*

"Hannah, I think you were on to something," I say. "Can you guys turn the lanterns back on?" I ask, putting one palm on either side of the line. My fingers twitch with anticipation. If I'm right...

"Whoa! Easy, tiger!" West grabs one of my wrists, panic written in his expression. "I thought we agreed smashing this is a bad idea."

"I'm not going to smash it," I say with a sly smile. "I'm going to open it. Watch."

With that, I take a deep breath and push on the glass. Ever so slowly, the two sides of the glass begin to move, opening outward just like the French doors in our kitchen at home. The thin line widens. First an inch, then two. Before we know it, we're standing in front of a space large enough for all of us to fit through.

We're also standing in front of the key.

CHAPTER FOURTEEN
START WITH THE KNICKKNACKS

"The door was here all along," West muses. "Which means we didn't need to worry about patterns or pulling down boxes to begin with. We could've just walked through to the other side and searched those boxes until we found the key."

The thought is maddening.

"The path is quite clear to reaching the key," I say. "The riddle told us the answer. Glass is clear."

Hannah bolts through the glass door and skids to a stop just short of the key. Her hand is outstretched, but she makes no move to pick it up.

"What are you doing?" I ask.

"Exercising good judgment. I'm going to work on it from now on." She waits until all three of us are surrounding the key, then gently nudges it with her toe. Nothing happens. "No more dumb decisions for me!"

West nods in approval. "I like this new Hannah."

Hannah beams. "You liked the old Hannah too. Don't lie."

"I wasn't saying I didn't like the old Hannah. Swear. I just meant that it's good you *probably* aren't going to do something that will get us killed in here," West answers with a smirk.

"*Probably*?" Hannah asks incredulously.

Even though he said it to be funny, something about West's comment bothers me. I've never felt unsafe in an escape room. Annoyed, yeah. But not unsafe. Knowing we don't have a clear exit from this house right now makes me anxious. It doesn't help that we're out in the country either. The farmhouses we saw definitely aren't close enough to hear us scream.

West must catch my frown because he pats me on the back. "We're going to be okay. And we're going to find that treasure and help your dad. If it exists, we aren't walking out of here without it."

"But to do that, we have to move faster." Hannah looks at her phone. "At some point our parents will expect us to have our phones back, and we've already been in here more than an hour."

The realization is like a punch to my gut. I knew we spent too long in these first two rooms, but I didn't know it was that much. And since we don't know how many other rooms there are in between us and the treasure, it's impossible to calculate our odds of succeeding. Too many variables.

Dropping down to the floor, I lower my head and look at the key from the side while West holds a lantern out to illuminate it. "Looks like a normal key. And since it fell out of the box, I don't think it could be tied to anything in this room."

"Sounds safe to me," West says. He reaches down and gives the key one more little nudge before finally picking it up. We stand still, looking around the room in silence to make sure that moving the key didn't trigger anything. With how wacky these triplets were, nothing would surprise me now.

With a calming breath, West unlocks the door with the etched deck of cards symbol on it. It creaks open, sending a nervous chill through me. *Whatever it is, we got this*, I tell myself.

My eyes widen as I take in the scene on the other side of the door. It's dark, so I can't make out everything, but I can tell it's much, *much* larger than I expected it to be. As big as the Circus Room at least.

"Holy cow," West starts, then trails off as he fumbles with the lanterns hooked over his wrist. Sliding one off, he hands it to Hannah. "This is huge. Let's find a place to put the lanterns down so we can figure out what we're dealing with."

We take our first careful steps in. The wooden floor squeaks and groans. I flip my phone light on just long enough to scan the area. Again, it's totally different from the last room we were in. The Circus Room was bright and exhilarating, the Box Room was dark and maddening, and this room, this room is...elegant?

A large chandelier hands from the ornate gold ceiling. Cobwebs are stretched across it, half covering the hundreds of little crystals that twinkle in my phone light. There's a fireplace at the far end of the room—one big enough to hold a whole firepit instead of just a few logs—and the walls are lined with shelves. Bookshelves. They stretch from the floor up to the ceiling, and there isn't one square inch that's empty. A ladder that slides from side to side is sitting at one end of each of the shelves, and clusters of armchairs and tables are scattered around the room.

"There must be hundreds of books in here," Hannah says, running her hand over the multicolored spines. "No, thousands."

West rubs at his face. "That means thousands of places to hide clues. I bet that some of these books are fake." He slowly slides one off the shelf. The book cracks as he opens it, revealing actual pages. "Well, this one is real, but no way they all are."

My shoulders sag. West is 100 percent right. A lot of escape rooms have features like hollowed-out books. They love to stash clues inside them. Codes, keys, riddles, you name it, and we've found it inside a book before.

Ugh. What if we have to check all of these? There isn't enough time.

"This feels like a rich person's house," I say with a laugh. Not like I'd know what a rich person's house looks like, but a girl can imagine. If I had lots of money, I wouldn't even want a mansion. I'd just want the house we already have. I'd buy it back from the bank and then stick my tongue out at them for being so mean to begin with.

The triplets pop into my head again. The article said that Karl might've studied literature and worked at a bookstore. Did he design this room? Perhaps libraries were his happy place, so he created one here? As frustrating as the triplets' funhouse is, I like the idea. No matter how bad things are at home, I can always distract myself with books. Reading about different people in different places makes me feel better. Maybe books did that for him when he was an orphan too.

"I say we start with the random stuff," Hannah says, gently tapping on a vase. "There are a lot of little knickknacks on these shelves. Let's check those first. We can save a lot of time if the key is hidden in one of those and not a book."

I consider this, realizing as I turn a full circle around the room that something is missing. "Um, hold up. Does anyone see a door?"

West looks startled as he spins his own circle to look. "No. You guys know what this means, right?"

"Hidden passages," Hannah and I say at the same time.

"Bingo," he answers. "We might not even be looking for a key in this room."

Aaaand this just got a lot more complicated.

Hidden passages in escape rooms are usually triggered by something. Moving or pushing an item, entering a code, or even just stepping in the right spot—like the clown in the Circus Room! With a room as big as this one though, it's going to be hard to find the trigger.

"Most common triggers are pulling books from shelves, entering codes into phones, and moving paintings," West recites, ticking off the items on his fingers like a list.

I don't know why I ask it, but I do. "How do you know that?"

"I read it in an article." He says this quietly and then refocuses on the books.

West always gets like this when the topic of his memory comes up. Hannah and I like to tease him about it, mostly because we're jealous, but sometimes West acts super weird. Like he's embarrassed or something. I don't get it. If I could remember as much as he does, I'd be a straight A student! I'd also be able to win pretty much every argument I have with Sean.

Hannah stuffs a new stick of gum in her mouth and grins. "Sounds boring, but I'm glad you read it, because that gives us a place to start!"

"Right! There's only one painting—the one above the fireplace. We could start there, and if it's a bust, at least we can mark that off the list," I suggest.

"Good thinking. And there is a phone over there," Hannah says, pointing to a small wooden table in the corner of the room. On top lies one of those old-fashioned phones with the cord. "Maybe we keep our eyes open for any sets of numbers that could be entered into that."

And just like that, we have a plan.

West pushes a leather armchair over to the fireplace and climbs up on it so he can reach the painting. Then he looks back down at us. "Are we all in agreement that I should move this painting?"

I nod. Hannah does the same. West grips the sides of the painting and tries to pull it from the wall. When it doesn't move, he gives us a look. It's the look of a guy who knows something is up. Normal paintings come off walls when they're pulled. This one must not be normal.

With a grunt, he rotates the painting upward from the left side like he's turning a steering wheel.

Just when I think nothing else is going to happen, a clinking sound starts up in the fireplace. It sounds like a roller coaster when you're on the way up a big hill.

Clink, clink, clink, GRIND.

West jumps off the armchair, and all three of us stare into the fireplace. The stone wall at the back has opened up.

I can't help it. I cheer. For once we caught a little good luck in this place. Finding the hidden passage in just one try is not only exciting, but it will also help us make up the time we lost in the first two rooms.

"West, I officially promise to never tease you for that freaky memory of yours ever again," I say, hugging him. "It just majorly paid off."

He lets a smile take over his face for a fleeting moment. Then the serious look comes back. "We should go. We don't celebrate after every little find in an escape room, and we definitely shouldn't here."

He's right. Not that he's wrong very often.

Snatching up the lanterns, I run back to the fireplace. West and Hannah are shining their phone lights into the dark space behind it. Out of all the things I expect West to say right now, like *It's another room*, or *It's a tunnel*, what he actually says surprises me.

"It's... I think it's a slide."

CHAPTER FIFTEEN
LONG LIVE THE DELTAS

The slide is made of metal and has a small *W* engraved in the mouth of it. It isn't prominent like the etchings of the playing cards, wishbone, and compass we've seen in here. It's plain and small. Probably just some kind of stamp from the company that made the slide.

I peer down into the dark, wondering what little surprises the triplets have in store for us down there. Hopefully no more lipstick-wearing goats.

"I don't think this is the slide we saw when we got here. That one was curvy. This one looks like it goes straight down," Hannah muses.

"Um, I think one of you should go first this time. I

volunteered for the trapeze," I say. Just the memory of flying across that room gives me the chills all over again.

"Eh, why not?" West says, putting one foot in the slide. "I've had a nice life."

Hannah and I laugh. It wouldn't be so funny if someone else said it, but the way West says things—all flat and without smiling—makes it funnier. My dad once called it dry humor. I call it hilarious.

I shove a lantern into his hands. "Take this. Once your feet hit the ground, yell up so we can slide down."

With a nod, West flips on the lantern and scoots forward until he whooshes down. I can hear the sound of his jeans against the slide for what seems like a long, long time. When it finally stops, there's a rustling. Then finally, an "All clear!"

Hannah immediately scrambles into the slide with a loud whoop. Her blond hair has come loose from the ponytail and is hanging down her back, wild and half-tangled. She vanishes before I can even say, *See you at the bottom.* I can still hear the echo of her sliding when West starts yelling again.

"Stop! Don't come down! I'm going to try to climb back up!"

Wait, what? Climb back up?

There's a muffled *oomph* followed by voices. Hannah and West are talking, and they *don't* sound happy.

"What is going on down there?" I shout down the slide. My heart is starting to thump unnaturally fast again.

"Hello? Guys?" My voice cracks.

When no one responds, I shakily climb into the slide. I'm scared, but these are my best friends in the world. If something is wrong, I need to help them. Turning on the second lantern, I let it light up the metal walls as they whoosh by. The slide is steeper than I expected it to be, so I build up speed fast. Finally, it spits me out onto a wood floor.

In the Box Room.

THE BOX ROOM.

I stand up and blink at the boxes dangling overhead. At the taxidermy goat. At West and Hannah, also gaping at the exact same room that just cost us so much time. And now we're right. Back. In it.

"I don't get it," I say, standing up and brushing the dust off my pants. "Why didn't you guys answer me? And why are we here again?"

West's jaw twitches. "I didn't answer because Hannah was chewing me out. Also, this makes no sense. We just slid down like an entire floor, but the Box Room was *upstairs* on the same level as the library. How is possible that we could land in here?"

I see what he means now. We were just on the same floor

as the Box Room. Sliding down this far and ending up in that same room isn't possible.

"This can't be the Box Room," Hannah says. She points to the glass barrier in the middle. "See how that's closed? And there aren't any boxes smashed on the floor or moved? This is a different room that just *looks* like the Box Room."

I gasp. A second Box Room? That's downright evil.

"I think you're right. This has to be a copy of the Box Room." At this realization, he groans. "Sucks because I liked the Circus Room better. Wish the triplets had stuck us back in there instead."

"Same," I look around, realizing that in this version of the Box Room, we're starting on the opposite side. Sure enough, the same deck of cards emblem is etched into the wood. The glass barrier in the center of the room is separating us from the goat head and the smaller door.

I immediately head for the barrier. It was unlocked in the original Box Room. Maybe it's unlocked in this one too!

Finding the barely-there seam in the glass, I put my palms on either side and press. Nothing. Not even a wiggle. I try again, this time pressing harder. Still nothing.

"It's locked, isn't it?" West asks, dismayed.

"Yup. If this is anything like the original Box Room, we're in trouble," I say pointing to the other side. "That little door on the other side had bricks behind it the first time. Remember? And I don't see another exit."

Hannah's face falls. Turning on her heel, she starts crawling into the slide. "I'm going to go back up this way. No way am I pulling those stupid boxes down again just to find a key that will get us nowhere!"

Her sneakers squeak against the metal as she climbs a few feet up, loses her footing, then slips and tumbles back down.

"It's too steep," she moans. "What are we going to do?"

"What the triplets wanted us to do," West answers. "This is probably a punishment for taking the wrong secret passage upstairs. We have to complete this room again and get back up there somehow."

The little clock inside me is ticking so loud I could cry. We're making too many mistakes. I don't like to admit it, but we've quit escape rooms before. When we knew we couldn't succeed or our time was bad, we stopped.

Maybe this is one of those times.

"If you guys had stopped fighting long enough to answer me when I was calling down, maybe you could have kept me from following you," I grumble. "I could have looked for the correct passage while you two found your way back to me."

Annoyance rolls around in me. I know Hannah and

West mean well, but sometimes their bickering makes things so much harder than they need to be.

"No way. We're supposed to stick together, remember? You said so yourself." Hannah looks at me pointedly. "Besides, this place is wacky. If we split up, there's a chance we could get separated. Permanently!"

Permanently separated. No, thank you. I imagine myself in ten years, covered in dust like the giant chandelier in the library. Maybe Art Conley and William Taters were lucky they got caught after all. At least they didn't get lost in this place and turn into mummies.

West paces the length of the room. "Let's just do this fast and find the way back upstairs."

"Fast? How is that possible?" I ask, gesturing to the boxes hanging overhead. "This took us forever before. I can't even begin to remember the order we chose the boxes in." My breath is coming out in fast, shallow pants now, and I realize I'm panicking.

Hannah wraps an arm around me, but West stalks off, his expression stormy. He quickly begins counting the boxes, then suddenly goes still like one of those hunting dogs that point at raccoons and squirrels and stuff.

Without warning, he reaches up and pulls the box down. A box on the other side falls and breaks open, revealing...

A key.

My mouth flops open. Hannah gasps, then immediately starts coughing.

"How...how did you do that?" I stammer, whacking Hannah on the back until a wad of chewed-up gum flies out of her mouth. "I know you have a good memory and all, but that was pretty much magic."

He shrugs. "Lucky, I guess."

"Lucky, my big toe!" Hannah exclaims. She opens a new stick of gum, shoving it in her mouth before she even fully stops coughing. "You just counted those boxes and decided on that one!"

A soft thunk comes from the center of the room. West shoulders past Hannah and me, cheeks flushed, to push on the glass barrier. This time, it opens.

"Holy moly! West!" Hannah screeches.

"That...that was... I don't even know what that was. Seriously, how are you doing this?" I'm sputtering, but I can't help it. I've seen West do some pre-tty amazing things before. He's found hidden passages in record time, decoded clues that neither Hannah or I could make sense of, and one time, he even figured out that we needed to use a fishing pole hanging above a fireplace to snag a key locked just out of reach. He's brilliant. But this is beyond that.

West ignores me. He's on the other side of the glass barrier now, moving like a character in fast-forward.

I grab his shoulder. "West. Stop. What's wrong?"

"Nothing," he spits out. "Let's just keep moving."

I shake my head. "Agreed, but this isn't nothing. You just saved the day. Why aren't you happy about that?"

"Because it's not as fun for me as it is for you," he snaps, then looks sorry. "I mean, the way my brain works is a problem sometimes. I know it seems cool, and yeah, maybe what I did just now helped us, but it isn't always like this, you know?"

I nod out of instinct, but the truth is, I don't know. I have no idea what West is talking about.

He leans against the wall, then slowly sinks down until he's sitting. "Look, Hannah isn't the only one who has been keeping secrets. I guess I have too."

"Okay," I say quietly. "Is this about you remembering which box it was?"

He nods but doesn't speak.

"I guess I don't understand what's so bad about having a good memory," I tell him. "What you just did was amazing."

"That's the problem. It's not *just* a good memory. It's a pain in the butt." He drops his head into his hands and scrubs at his hair. "I remembered that box and that pattern, and I'll probably still remember it months from today. Maybe I'll be brushing my teeth, and that pattern will pop into my head. Or maybe I'll be trying to read a book and *boom!* Pattern."

I slide down next to him and sit. "Okay. I guess I can see how that would be annoying."

"It's not just annoying," he grumbles.

"You're embarrassed," Hannah says. It's not a question either. It's a statement, like she knows. "I mean, I wouldn't be embarrassed if I had your memory, but I know that's why I didn't tell you guys about failing out of dance. I was ashamed."

"I'm tired of it," West admits. "It's not just that I can't forget things the way a normal person does. It's that once people figure out that I have a different memory, they make a huge deal of it. Like you guys just did."

I look down at the splinters of wood on the floor, realizing maybe I did go a little overboard. It's just that I don't have a skill like that. I don't know anyone else who does.

"Once they get over the shock, they immediately think it's unfair. That *I'm* somehow unfair." He looks up, his eyes crinkled with worry. "Did I ever tell you that I won the school spelling bee in fifth grade? I did. It should have been exciting. Instead, it was terrible."

Hannah's eyes widen. "I remember that! You didn't go to the awards ceremony, but you never told me why."

"I didn't go because my neighbor Buddy Travers knew

about my memory. Our moms were friends back then. Anyway, he was mad that he came in third and ended up telling some other kids. They said I was a cheater and that I shouldn't have been allowed to do the spelling bee to begin with." West looks up, his hair a wild mass standing on top of his head. "I couldn't go take that award knowing that's what they thought."

Hannah scowls. "I didn't hear anything about that."

"Do you blame them? You were a foot taller than all the boys back then and my best friend. My very protective best friend. I wouldn't have wanted to make you mad either," he says, laughing weakly. "Anyway, having a memory like mine doesn't mean it's easier for me to learn stuff. I have to work as hard as everyone else! I just remember it longer."

I open my mouth to say something, but West holds a hand up. "Before you say that I shouldn't care what other people think, remember that you recorded the same video like *two dozen times* for TikTok last week. You care. Everyone does. It's why I can't ace too many tests or raise my hand too often in class."

The pain in West's voice breaks my heart. All this time I thought having a memory like his would be amazing. Now I realize for him, it's a curse. It's like me with statistics and probabilities. Only I can control it. Shut it off if I really need to. I wish West could too.

"So you hide it then? Hide how good your memory is so people don't judge you?" I ask.

"I have to."

"This reminds me of Peter Parker," Hannah says. "You know, Spiderman? He has to keep his powers hidden too!"

West bursts into laughter. "Um, yeah. I wouldn't call this a power. Not unless I wake up and can also shoot webs or stick to buildings."

I'm so glad to see him smiling again that I smile too. "Remember how you told Hannah she should never worry about being weak or letting us down?"

West meets my eyes. "Yeah."

"Well, you should never worry that we'll judge you. You have a good memory, who cares? You still smell like an old dirty sock after gym class and snore when you fall asleep on the bus after field trips."

"Oh! And don't forget how he always eats more than his third of the fries at the hot dog stand," Hannah adds. "You and I hardly get any thanks to this maniac!"

"What we're trying to say is that everyone has strengths and weaknesses. Your memory is awesome. Don't let other people convince you that it's something bad." I wait to see how he reacts, hoping that for once, West just agrees.

He cracks a smile. "All right. All right. But you guys went

a little far with all that *he stinks and eats like a pig* stuff, don't you think?"

"That depends. Did it work?" I wait for his answer, then jostle into him with my shoulder. "Seriously. Anyone who thinks you're a cheater doesn't really know you."

West's head droops back down again, but this time it isn't in defeat. It's relief. I don't know how I didn't notice it before, but West has been carrying around this worry for a long, long time. And if anyone knows how much worry can eat away at a person, it's me.

I point to the small door. "Ready to open it?"

"What are the odds it's filled with bricks like the other one was?" he asks.

Shrugging, I stand up. "Pretty good, but that doesn't mean it's hopeless. The probability of three math nerds who all love escape rooms finding each other and being best friends probably wasn't good either. But we did."

"Long live the Deltas," Hannah says, holding out a hand to pull West up.

Long live the Deltas.

CHAPTER SIXTEEN
AND SOMETHING YOU KNOW

Hannah and I crowd around West as he inserts the key into the lock on the small door. Tossing a nervous look back at us, he unlocks it and pulls the door open.

Another brick wall.

"Well, that's just great," West says. "The only obvious exit in here, and it's not real."

He sinks further back on his haunches, clearly exasperated.

"I'm really starting to dislike the triplets," Hannah says, plucking the gum from her mouth. "Because this is mean."

With that, she reaches out and sticks her newest piece of chewed-up gum on the bricks. I make a gagging face. Even though I agree with her that the triplets' funhouse isn't all that fun, it's a disgusting thing to do.

"Hey," she says, holding her palm in front of the door like she's warming it by a fire. "Do you guys feel that? That air?"

West and I stick our own hands out. Sure enough, there's a breeze.

"It's coming from the door!" I say excitedly. "You know what this means, right?"

Instead of answering, West starts knocking on the bricks. They don't sound dull like real bricks would; they sound hollow.

"They're not real!" West and I shout in unison.

I search the edges of the fake bricks to see if there's something I can pull on. An edge, a corner, anything. When I get my thumb and index finger around one of them, I don't waste any time in pulling.

Rather than just that brick coming out, the whole panel of fake bricks pulls off the doorway. It's light, nothing more than textured plastic painted brown and red. Musty air flies out, peppering us with dust and bits of cobwebs. The wall and ceiling are rounded and made of something that looks like hardened clay. Stairs lead up into the pitch black.

A tunnel!

"Pretty sure it's your turn to go first," I say to Hannah, nudging her forward. "Plus, you're the one who figured this out. Wanna lead the way?"

"Absolutely!" Grinning, Hannah snags a lantern from the floor and holds it out in front of her. She hunches down to step through the small door, then grunts.

"Oof, it's tight in here. And there's something written on the wall." She stops a few steps up and turns sideways to cast her light over the painted letters. "*The path you last chose led you astray. Choose wrong again, and blue skies will turn gray. There is one direction forward, one way you must go. Through locked rooms is a victory and something you know.*"

Hannah stops reading.

I'm so excited I'm quivering. "Does that say what I think it does? I mean, it sounds like a hint about the treasure, doesn't it?"

I replay the words in my head. *And something you know.* West said that the triplets talked about the hidden treasure when they were getting ready to open the house, before one of them died. Could that be what the riddle is talking about? Did they expect everyone who entered the funhouse to know about the treasure? I imagine it sitting in the final room waiting for us. Maybe it's a chest like you'd see on a pirate ship. Or maybe it's just a plain brown bag filled with money. Whatever it is, I want it.

No, I *need* it.

West sighs. "It sounds like it could be about the treasure,

yeah, but knowing the triplets, it could be a hint about anything. *Something you know* is pretty vague."

Brushing a cobweb out of her hair, Hannah nods. "I think you're both right. The only way to find out for sure is to keep going."

She turns around and continues up the steps, motioning for us to follow. I go next. West trails in the back, running his fingers over the message scratched into the walls.

"It's...getting...tighter," Hannah grunts out. "Seriously, I feel like the walls are closer up here."

I round my back even more to stay hunched over. This time it's not an optical illusion; the walls are definitely closing in. I can feel them brushing against my arms and even the top of my shoulders.

I lift my right foot, but I can't find the step. It's shorter than the last one. Much shorter.

"What is up with these steps? They're so small now." I pause to look back at West, but it's too narrow for me to turn around. "West, are you okay back there?"

"Other than the fact that I'm already crawling, yeah. I'm okay. You guys?"

Hannah doesn't answer. I crane my neck up to look at her, realizing that the passage ahead of her has gotten so small she's on her belly. The sound of her lantern scraping across the ground echoes through the space, raising hairs on the back of my neck.

"Get down as flat as you can, guys. The stairs are gone, and it's like a ramp or something up here." Hannah blows out a puff of air. I'm glad she went first. Out of the three of us, she's always the most fearless.

Flattening myself as much as possible, I use my arms and legs to keep pushing my body upward. The ramp isn't steep, but it's slick and difficult to get a grip on anything. With my next push forward, my forehead connects with something hard.

Hannah's shoe.

"Hey, keep moving. I just about concussed myself on your sneaker," I grind out.

"I can't," she says. Her voice is strained. "The tunnel ended. There's gotta be an exit here somewhere, but I can't see it."

Great. Just great. We're stuck on our bellies in a dark narrow tunnel, and there's no way out. Just the thought makes me itch and cough.

"Do what we always do, Hannah," West calls out. "Start pushing on everything. Push *hard* and try every spot of the wall."

There's a swishing noise followed by a knock. Then another knock. Hannah twists and turns her slender frame around in the tight space, looking for a way out.

"Oh!" she exclaims. "I think I found something! There's a spot where the wall wiggles!"

I hear scraping, like metal on metal, then a loud thump. "Ow!"

"Hannah?" I yell.

The scraping sound is back, and Hannah's light suddenly vanishes. Sticking an arm out in front of me, I wave my hand blindly around in the dark, hoping to connect with her shoe again. The area is empty though. No Hannah.

My blood turns to ice.

"Hannah!" I yell louder this time. West yells too.

"I'm all right. But stay where you are! Don't move!" Hannah's voice comes through the walls, but it's soft. She's definitely not in the tunnel with us anymore. The thought frightens me.

I freeze in place. Not that there's much choice. West sputters into a fit of coughing behind me, then moans.

"Any day now, Banana," he shouts.

I laugh. *Banana* has been one of West's nicknames for Hannah since I moved here. He doesn't use it very often, but when he does, I kinda love it. West is serious so often that it's a relief to hear him be silly—even if he is doing it while we are cramped in a death tunnel.

Something crawls across the top of my hand. I shake it

off, trying to stay calm even though I'm not. Dark, scary tunnels are one thing. Creepy crawlies are another thing entirely.

The scraping sound returns. Then, an opening appears in the wall. Light fills the tunnel again. It's from Hannah's lantern.

"Oh, thank god," she hisses. "That was tricky. Here, grab my hand and I'll pull you guys out."

Slithering forward, I take her hand. Hannah starts gently pulling. I reach the door and tumble out, realizing too late that there's a drop.

I land on my shoulder, grateful that it wasn't my head. "Sheesh, Hannah! Thanks for the warning!"

She laughs. "I'm sorry, okay! Let me help West."

While she's pulling West out of the wall, I look around. We're back in the library, but the "door" we spilled out of is one of the bookshelves. Wow. It's so realistic-looking I never would've suspected it was fake.

Suddenly, I remember West.

"West, be careful when you get to the..."

THUD.

"Opening," I finish.

West hits the floor with a grunt.

"Too late," he says, standing up and brushing off. He looks around the room, arching an eyebrow. "At least we made it back. We just can't make that mistake of going the wrong way again."

"Agreed," I say. "But how do we avoid it?"

"I don't know. But we don't have time to try every wrong passage in here."

We definitely don't have time to try that. For one, our parents will expect us to check in soon. When we don't, they'll worry. Even worse, I'm beginning to think we didn't plan quite as well as we thought we did. My stomach is growling, and other than the granola bars we wolfed down on the train here, I didn't pack anything to eat. Not even a lousy bag of chips. What will we do if we're still in here hours from now? If we can't find the exit at all? I imagine having to sleep in here tonight and frown.

"There must be a clue about the correct passage somewhere." West continues, gently tipping a vase and examining the bottom.

Or a clue about the wrong passage. Uh-oh.

"Oh no," I say, a terrible thought slamming into me. "I think I might have really messed up."

"How?" West asks.

"I think I saw a clue and didn't know it was a clue. When we found the slide behind the fireplace, I noticed that there was a small *W* stamped on it." I walk over there and gesture at it. "See there? I thought it was just branding from the company that built the slide, but now I wonder if it stands for *wrong*. As in, *Wrong way, dummies.*"

My shoulders sag. One of the biggest rules of escape rooms is to pay attention to details! If something looks out of place, it probably is. Even a rookie would know this. I should've mentioned the *W* right when I saw it. Now we're all being punished.

I. Am. An. Idiot.

Hannah has a finger on her chin, apparently deep in thought. "Maybe. But if that's true, then you still figured something out. If the *W* on this slide stands for *wrong*, then that would mean we would need to find a passage marked with an *R* for *right*."

"Hey, back up a second. The door we came through had a deck of cards on it. Remember?" West asks. "The whole theme of the Box Room was strategy, and those cards were our clue. Maybe we missed a symbol in the painting that would tell us what the theme of *this* room is. If we know that, it might give us an idea of how to solve it."

Hannah and I sprint to the fireplace. Hannah climbs up on the armchair and examines the painting. "Yes!" she points at a swirl of red. "Look at this! Doesn't that look like a compass to you?"

It looks *exactly* like a compass.

"Oh man," West mutters. "This is starting to make more sense. Remember the riddle in the tunnel? It said, *There is one* direction *forward*. I think that's theme of this room. Directions! We need to pick the correct one—north, south, east, or west."

"Ooh! Maybe the *W* in the slide doesn't stand for *wrong* after all," I say. "If the theme of this room is direction, maybe the *W* stands for *west*! If that's the west passage, then we know there are at least three more—north, south, and east!"

"Yes!" Hannah looks at the fireplace slide. "I guess the big question is, where are the other passages, and which one is correct? The riddle in the tunnel was pretty clear that there's only one right direction. Anyone have a clue if it's north, east, or south?"

West and I shake our heads somberly.

Sweat beads on my head. I am *so* lost. *Lasers and Lava* was nothing compared to this. Maybe the Deltas have finally met their match.

CHAPTER SEVENTEEN
BEAUTY AND THE BOOKSHELVES

"What was that list of things you said before, West? The most common things that open secret passageways?" Hannah asks. "Maybe we go back to that. At least we won't be burning more time."

West's eyes are glazed, like he's on another planet. Hazard of being this deep in an escape room. Eventually you lose track of what's real and what's not. "Oh, yeah. Sorry, I was zoned out. The most common triggers are pulling books off shelves, putting codes into phones, and moving paintings."

All three of us immediately look at the phone in the corner. Hannah saw it back when we moved the painting. Maybe we should've tried it first.

Hannah skips over to the phone and looks from me to West.

"I say try it. See if it says anything," West suggests.

When I agree with him, Hannah lifts the part of the phone you put on your ear and presses it to her head. Then she begins to recite what she's hearing.

"*Welcome to the library. There is one direction forward, one way you must go. Through locked rooms is a victory and something you know.*"

"Same message that was in the tunnel we crawled through to get back in here," I say. "So, our theory about needing to pick a direction has to be right."

Hannah suddenly holds a finger in the air. "*Now, please enter your answer.*"

West rushes to her side and tries to press his ear to the phone. Hannah swats him away.

"Wait, did it say that just now? It said, '*Enter your answer*'?" he asks.

Setting the phone back down on the large part that is plugged into the wall, Hannah nods. "Sure did. Looks like your research was right and this *could* be the way to trigger another secret passage."

"What kind of answer, though?" I pose.

"Not a number answer, that's for sure. There aren't even numbers on this thing." Hannah points down at the rotary phone. It's the kind that has a circular thing you use a finger to spin when you want to call someone. No one uses them anymore, but we've seen them in escape rooms a lot of times. "They're letters instead."

"Okay, sounds like we need to enter our answer on this and it's a word, not numbers." I stare down at the collection of letters on the phone, imagining what words we could make with them.

NTSEWHOURA

"News, whose, rose, ours, ran," West pauses, scowling. "This is impossible. Even though there are only ten letters here, there are a ton of words we can make with those."

There is one direction forward. The clue surges into my head again. That's it!

"We need to enter one of the directions," I say, examining the phone. I use my finger to mentally spell out north, south, and east, pumping my fist when I realize that there are just enough letters to do it. "Yes! The hint clearly says there is only one direction forward. There are enough letters to spell all four directions here."

West perks up. "And we know the answer isn't west, since that was the wrong passage." He glances around, his eyebrows scrunching up again. "Problem is, I don't know how to figure out which of the other three directions is right."

"I'm not up for guessing," Hannah says. "If we end up in the Box Room a third time, I'll go crazy."

"Same, but that isn't going to happen. The answer has to be in this room somewhere. Everything we needed to get out of the Circus Room was in there. Same for the Box Room. I guess we just start looking?" I suggest.

"Already on it!" Hannah chirps.

I whirl around and gasp. She's halfway up one of the rolling ladders and still climbing. "Hannah! Be careful!"

She swings an arm and leg off the side of it, laughing. The ladder glides a few feet to the side. "Do I look like Belle?"

Even though she's making me nervous, I laugh with her. Hannah loves Disney movies, and *Beauty and the Beast* has always been one of her favorites.

"Sure. Just remember there's no signal in here to call an ambulance if you break your neck!" I turn away, shaking my head when Hannah begins to belt out the lyrics to her favorite song from the movie.

Always entertaining, that Banana is.

Since West is searching through the vases, globes, and books on his side of the room, I decide to focus on the floor. We've been in escape rooms before where there are trapdoors and secret codes hidden under rugs. I lift the edge of the rug, exhaling out my frustration when I find nothing underneath but a few dead bugs, some lint, and more dust than my already twitchy nose can handle.

"I know we've said this before, but the triplets really were something," Hannah calls down. "The books up here are arranged strangely."

"It's called alphabetical," West says, not even turning around. Still, I can see the smirk on his face.

"Very funny," she answers with a huff. "Aren't most books in libraries arranged according to the author's last name? These are totally disorganized. They aren't even separated by what they're about. This book is about cooking with noodles, this one is about narwhals, and this one is about the benefits of napping. Weird."

"Eh, it's not that weird. This isn't a real library. The triplets probably didn't care what order the books were in," I say.

West tips a vase upside down then sets it back on the shelf. "But the rest of the house has been so detailed. Seems a little strange that they'd be sloppy with this."

I think on this for a minute, realizing he's right. Even the taxidermy goat in the Box Room was a clue. At least it held one. That means there's a good probability that the disorganized books are a clue too. I look up at where Hannah is sliding across the floor on the ladder, thinking about the book topics she read off to us.

Cooking with Noodles

Narwhals

Benefits of Napping

I suck in an excited breath. The books aren't disorganized at all! In fact, they're perfectly organized!

"*N!*" I shout. "*Noodles. Narwhals. Napping.* The main topic of all those books is something that begins with an *N!*"

West and Hannah look at each other, then scramble into a flurry of movement. Hannah climbs down from the ladder. West starts reading off the titles of the books that line the wall he's been searching.

"Oceans, ornithology, ophthalmology," he stops to take a breath. "Octopi. Yeah, all the books on these shelves are about something that begins with the letter *O.*"

And suddenly I feel like we're in an episode of *Sesame Street*.

"I bet if I look at the books on both sides the fireplace, they'll start with..." I start.

"*R* and *T*," Hannah finishes for me. "That just leaves..."

West grins as he pulls a book down from the final wall and holds it up for us to see. "*H.* As in, *Hippos and Their Habitat.*"

North. The topics of the books in the room spell out the direction north.

The three of us race back to the telephone. West lifts the ear part and starts carefully dialing. *N-O-R-T-H.*

"Congratulations!" The voice is loud enough to hear even though my ear isn't to the phone.

There's a clink followed by a burst of something falling from the ceiling. Confetti? I shield my eyes and look up, stunned to see that there was a trapdoor hidden in the ornate ceiling. Instead of opening up like the ones we've seen in the floor of escape rooms, this one opens down. The door is hanging, still swaying from being released.

"That confetti better be a good sign," West says. His expression is serious, but his hair is speckled in a rainbow of glitter.

I laugh. "You look ridiculous. Like you belong back down in the Circus Room."

Bending down, he shakes it out of his hair. "Ha-ha. Make fun of the confetti-covered guy. C'mon. The confetti is cool, but we can't let it distract us."

Following West to the ladder Hannah was on before, I shake her arm. "Can you believe this? We just beat two rooms that no one else has been in before!"

"Three, if you count the copy of the Box Room," she says with a dazzling grin. "And yeah, I can believe it. When the Deltas decide to do something, they do it."

Truth. And I've decided we're 100 percent, no questions asked, without a doubt, absolutely, positively going to get. That. Treasure.

CHAPTER EIGHTEEN

ROME WASN'T BUILT IN A DAY

Hannah crawls up the ladder first.

"I want adventure," she croons.

"Stuff it, Hannah," West yells. "We don't have time for you to reenact *Beauty and the Beast* right now. It wasn't even good the first time."

Hannah stops climbing. She turns around, eyes flashing. "What did you say?"

I get on my tiptoes so I'm close to his ear. "Abort! Abort!"

West clears his throat. "I said it was too good the first time. Don't want to tarnish the memory of it."

"Nice save," I whisper.

Lifting her chin up as if she accepts his lie, Hannah starts moving again. When she gets to the trapdoor in the ceiling, she stops and unclips the lantern from the carabiner attached to her waist.

Hannah holds the lantern with one hand and the ladder with the other. Lifting the lantern up into the ceiling, she takes one more tentative step and gasps.

"What?" I call up to her. "What is it?"

"Is it the treasure?" West shouts.

I imagine crawling up the ladder and landing in an enormous pile of gold coins. No, not gold coins. Hundred-dollar bills. Thousand-dollar bills! Wait, do those even exist?

"No, it's not the treasure," Hannah calls down. She uses her arms to push herself up into the hole and then looks down at us. "But it's really wild. Come on!"

Grunting, I climb through the trapdoor and use my arms to drag myself fully up. Then I turn on my lantern.

After the trapeze in the Circus Room, the goat in the Box Room, and the fireplace slide in the library, I didn't think it was possible to be surprised anymore.

I was wrong.

"What is this place?" Hannah says in a whisper. She sounds like she's in church, half-afraid to speak too loudly.

I turn a circle, taking in my surroundings. The first thing I notice is the large white pillars that run from the floor up to the ceiling. *Doric.* I remember the word from history. We studied Rome for a week and learned all about their architecture. Before that, I thought a column is just a column, but no. They had different kinds, all of them pretty.

West pulls himself up through the hole, then immediately closes the door again. "I think we should keep that closed so none of us accidentally fall back through." Suddenly, his eyes widen as if he's just noticed what he's surrounded by.

Pillars, yeah, but also statues. Dozens and dozens of statues. White marble covered in dust and cobwebs. There are statues of men, women, children, and even a dog. Some of them are on pedestals on the floor, but many of them are mounted in nooks set into the walls. I stare at them, mesmerized.

Meanwhile, West looks bothered.

"What's wrong?" I ask. "Don't you think this is cool?"

"Yeah, it is," he answers. "It just reminds me of this wax museum I visited with my parents once. We didn't know it, but it was all Halloween-themed. Had figures of Jason and Michael Myers, Ghostface, you know. Those guys. But some of them were real people just standing still and pretending to be made of wax."

I immediately make a face. I don't like where this is going.

"Anyway, since they were all so realistic, we couldn't tell the difference between the real people and the wax ones. That is, until the real people jumped out at us."

Hannah snaps a bubble, laughing. "That sounds like a blast to me."

"Sounds like a heart attack to me," I say.

West smiles. "I guess it was a little of both. This room, though, it gives me those vibes." He walks closer to one of the statues and looks into its face. "Even though these aren't painted, they still look like they could come to life."

I shake off the cold chill his words send through me. They are not coming to life. Nothing in here is coming to life. It's a funhouse, not a haunted house. "Good thing this place has been closed for so long. No chance of that."

Hannah pokes one in the eye. "Yeah, if this guy were real, these eye pokes would get him moving."

"Don't harass the statues, Hannah," I say, laughing. Sliding my phone out of my pocket, my heart sinks. We've been in here so long.

West bumps into me intentionally. "Now you're the one that looks freaked out."

I put my phone away and sigh. "Yeah, not by the statues though. I guess I'm just worried. Any of our parents could have tried to reach us by now. We don't even know where we are in the house. What if there are a ton of rooms left? What if we aren't even halfway done?"

West grips my shoulder and gives it a gentle shake. "Stop. We've been over this. If our parents try to reach us, they won't panic. They think we're in an escape room downtown. They won't expect an answer."

Right. I know this. Still, the thought is unsettling. Ever since Dad got sick, Mom needs more help. I do things around the house I never thought about doing before. Sometimes she even calls me from work to add another chore to my list. I'm not complaining; it's fine. It's just scary on a day like today when I know she can't find me if something random comes up.

Another terrible thought grips me. "What do we do when we have to pee in here?"

"If you have to pee," he starts, waving his hand across the room. "Then pee. We'll turn the other way."

"Like...on the floor? West! I'm not a schnauzer!"

He shrugs. "I'm just saying the triplets probably put a bathroom in here somewhere, but I doubt we're going to find it, so you might as well pick a corner and just do it."

I look around, horrified. Every floor in this place is filthy. Every corner filled with shadows and cobwebs. How could anyone pee in here and not be terrified?

My face must give away how I'm feeling, because Hannah hugs me. "Would it make you feel better to poke one of the statues?"

I laugh despite my nerves and the slight twinge in my bladder. "Sweet of you...well, sorta sweet...but no, thanks. I think the only thing that will make me feel better is if we figure out what we need to do in this room."

"Figured out one thing already," West says from the other end of the room. "This looks like an exit, but there's no handle and no lock."

Hannah and I walk over to meet him, weaving in and out of the statues. The door is actually two doors that meet in the middle. They're made of wood and have birds and trees carved into them. I think about how much Dad would like them. He's a nature guy, as he likes to say.

"No lock means no key," Hannah says, interrupting my thoughts. "Guess we're looking for another trigger that will open up that door."

"Wow," West says. "This place must've been cutting-edge back in the fifties. Trapdoors? Automatic doors? Hidden buttons and confetti in the ceiling? Too bad it never opened."

Too bad is right. Even though I'm a ball of nerves, this house is awesome. Room after room of puzzles, challenges, and even some danger. No way would an escape room featuring a trapeze be allowed now. Not that it should, but it did give me the chance to be brave for once. We all deserve to feel brave now and again.

"Hmmm, anyone have a theory on these?" Hannah points toward three empty pedestals. Each one is set into a different wall. "Maybe they didn't have a chance to finish this room?"

"It looks pretty finished to me," I say running a hand over the doors. Even specked with years of dirt and dust, it's beautiful. "No way they took time to have something like this carved but forgot three entire statues."

West paces between the pedestals. "Agreed. This room took some serious time. Rome wasn't built in a day, you know." He laughs at his own joke the way he always does back home.

I roll my eyes. "You sure do have the dad jokes locked down."

He puts a hand to his chest, looking offended. "Dad jokes? That was not a dad joke! It was hilarious."

"Hilarious if your idea of fun is watching the news," I fire back, fighting a smile.

"The empty pedestals are intentional. They have to be," Hannah suddenly says, interrupting us. Her voice is so loud that it startles me. West too.

"You mean, it could be part of the riddle," West asks. "Okay. Let's pretend the triplets left these three pedestals empty on purpose. What did they want us to do? Put statues on them?"

Even though he says this with a snort, as if it couldn't possibly be true, my stomach does a flip at the thought. The triplets *did* make us swing across a room with no safety harness and no net below us. Maybe they expect us to move these statues? I look around again, this time feeling less mesmerized and more overwhelmed. The statues may be pretty, but they look heavy.

"No. No way," Hannah squeaks. "They can't expect us to do that. These statues are ginormous! And there's only three of us!"

"There might not be a choice," I tell her, secretly terrified that this is it. The nail in the coffin. Every room in this house is harder than the last, and this one just might be the one that dooms us. "We had to escape the Box Room a second time, which proves that the triplets weren't really worried about people getting out of their funhouse quickly. They wanted them to have an experience. And moving these giant statues is *definitely* going to be an experience."

CHAPTER NINETEEN

OPERATION BEAT THE TRIPLETS

When I first heard that Dad was sick, that he had a condition that was never going to go away, I felt like someone knocked the wind out of me. Life just kept going on around us as if it didn't matter that my family was falling apart. Being stuck in this room while my hopes and dreams fizzle out like a soggy match isn't that different. Outside, the neighbors are probably cutting their lawns or taking walks or doing whatever it is they do on a normal day. Meanwhile we're struggling. Bad.

"There aren't any extra statues," West observes. "I mean, it's not like there's a pile of statues with no pedestals to choose from."

I try to pull myself out of my funk. Looking around, I see what he's saying. Every statue in the room is on a pedestal. "We need to move a statue from its current pedestal to one of these."

"No," Hannah says. "We need to move *three* statues from their current pedestals. The question is, which ones and how do we do it?"

I groan. When it comes to odds, this room is bad news. Too many choices, and none of them seem like a slam dunk.

The thoughts raging in my head are officially grim. That means it's time to launch *Operation Beat the Triplets*. The Deltas have made it this far and we can't quit now. "Spread out. Look for clues. In the last room, the answer depended on us paying attention to little things like the titles on the books. It could be something like that in here too."

West knocks on the wall beside him. "I'll start here. Hannah, you good taking that wall?"

"Yup! And Sarah—the last wall with the empty pedestal is all you."

I salute the two of them and head to my wall. I know it's impossible, but it feels like the statues are watching me, following me with their eyes. I pause and jab one.

"Sarah?" West says, cracking up. "What are you doing?"

"Just making sure," I answer. "I decided I'm with you. I don't like these very much."

Hannah makes a *tsk*ing sound from her side of the room. She's standing up on a pedestal with one of the statues, her arm casually draped around his shoulder. It looks extra funny since the statue is of a man with his fist raised to the sky in anger. "I think they're fun! Maybe after we get the treasure, we can find a way to get one of these home. I think it would look great in my room!"

West looks at her like she's suddenly speaking another language. "You want one of these for your room? What are you going to do with it, hang your jewelry on it?"

She shrugs. "No clue, but I would never be alone!"

The idea of one of these things in my room makes me shudder, but Hannah and I are different. I've grown up with Sean. Yeah, he burps and farts and makes a mess of our shared bathroom *all* the time, but he also sticks up for me and helps me when I need it. Hannah is an only child, so she's never had that. It probably made the whole dance thing that much harder to go through—being alone.

"I'm not up for stealing it, but if we find the treasure, I'll buy one for you. How about that?" I ask her.

Hannah smiles. "Deal."

I refocus on my statues and the wall I'm supposed to be searching, stopping when a loud crash rings out. West's head is tossed back, his hands covering it entirely.

"What happened?" Hannah asks.

"I was trying to see if the statues just *look* heavy. I thought maybe there's a chance they're actually made of papier-mâché or something like that. I started with the dog statue. Since it's the smallest, I thought I could lift it." He runs a hand through his hair, then bends down and starts rummaging through the chunks on the floor. "Turns out the statues aren't papier-mâché. The dog was heavy, and I lost control of it. I'm sorry, guys."

I make my way over to the mess. Jagged bits of doggie sculpture are everywhere. West turns them over one at a time, but there's nothing to see. No hidden words, letters, or even numbers. It's just a pile of plaster.

"Hey, that may not have been planned, but it wasn't a bad thing. Now we know we can't move any of these statues onto those empty pedestals. That dog was tiny. The human ones are four times the size."

"There are still two little kid statues," Hannah points out. "Think if we all work together, we could move those?"

"Probably, but we'd still be missing a third sculpture," I pose. I hate to say it, but the broken dog statue could be a bigger problem than I thought.

"This can't be the only way. The triplets wouldn't have created a room that's almost impossible for kids," Hannah says. She's not hugging a statue anymore. Now she's putting lip gloss on one.

Things are going downhill fast.

West suddenly jerks upright. "Wait! I just remembered

something! A friend from summer camp was telling me about an escape room he did once where they had to use weight to trigger something to happen. What if we don't need to put *statues* on the pedestals? What if any weight will work?"

"There *are* three pedestals," Hannah says with a twinkle in her eye. "And three of us."

I'm so excited I could scream. The triplets could easily have created this room with multiple solutions. If a group of adults came through who were strong and able to move the statues, great. But a group like us—younger and smaller—would've needed a second option. Our own body weight could be it!

The three of us race to the empty pedestals.

"On the count of three?" I ask.

West nods enthusiastically. "Yup. One..."

"Two," Hannah says.

I take a deep breath, lift my foot from the ground and say, "Three."

Then we each step onto our individual pedestals and wait for the wooden doors to pop open.

CHAPTER TWENTY
NOSE TO THE GRINDSTONE

The wooden doors do *not* pop open. I don't have time to feel annoyed about it, because I realize I'm moving. Not just me, West and Hannah too. Our pedestals are sinking.

Mine lowers about two inches, then stops. I stay still, unsure of how long our weight needs to stay in place to trigger the lock.

"Um, guys?" Hannah's voice breaks the silence. Her pedestal is lowering too, but it isn't stopping at the two inches. In fact, it isn't stopping at all!

"Our weight must have opened a secret passage!" West yells. He moves to leave his spot, then stops. "I don't think Sarah and I should come over there yet. Our pedestals must've been the buttons that activated yours. If we hop down, I'm afraid you'll stop."

I rub my hands together, partly because they're cold, but also because they're clammy again. "Way to go, Hannah! You found a new passage!"

She nods at me, but her expression isn't confident. She looks frightened as she continues to lower into the floor.

"I...I don't like this." Her voice cracks. "It doesn't feel right. I think I should try to climb out."

Just as the words leave her mouth, her face vanishes fully below the ground, and there's a new sound. A painful metal-on-metal sound that makes me cover my ears. Hannah screams.

I jump off my stand, no longer caring about the weight and the buttons. Racing over to the hole where Hannah's pedestal used to stand, my mouth falls open. A set of metal bars has slid across the circular opening, trapping her inside the cylinder.

"It's not a secret passage," I croak out. "It's a cage. West!"

West is already at my side, now covering the ear I just screamed in.

Hannah presses her face up to the bars. She looks angry. "You said this was a secret passage, Westley!"

He tosses his hands in the air. "I thought it was! I'm sorry!"

"I think we were supposed to use the statues after all," I

say. "Maybe the triplets thought using our own body weight was a shortcut, so they built in a little extra challenge to make things fair. Remember how we got sent to the copy of the Box Room because we chose the wrong secret passage? That was a punishment. I think this is a punishment too."

West's eyes are blazing "What a load of crap. This isn't fair at all."

It isn't fair, but I get it. The triplets gave us three small statues—two children and a dog. If West hadn't broken the dog, we would have had to wrestle the statues onto the empty pedestals. It would have been hard and taken a lot of teamwork. Time too. If we'd done that, none of us would be trapped right now. But we goofed up, and now we're paying the price.

Reaching down, I grip the bars and rattle as hard as I can. They don't budge.

"This is terrible! We weren't supposed to get separated, and now look! I'm stuck in the floor!"

I drop down onto my hands and knees so I'm closer to her. "Calm down, Hannah. We'll get you out. Do you have a lantern?"

She nods and begins to squirm around. "Yeah, but it's too tight down here for me to get it. It's hanging on my jeans again."

"Does that mean it's too dark to look around down there?" I continue.

"Look around at what?" she shouts. "It's practically a coffin! There's nothing to look at!"

"They knew," West says somberly. "They knew the only people who would make this mistake would be smaller and weaker. Kids. An adult probably wouldn't even fit down there."

I didn't even think of that. It makes me want to slap someone, namely the triplets.

West slides his lantern over to the bars. It flickers a few times. He swats it on the side, breathing a sigh of relief when it stays on. "Our batteries are probably dying. I didn't expect to use these so much in here."

"And I didn't expect to end up in a death hole, but guess what? Here I am!" Hannah snips. There's dirt on her forehead now, probably from smashing her face against the bars.

"It's not a death hole," I tell her. "In fact, the odds are slim that you die in there."

"But there's a chance?" She screeches.

Stop talking, Sarah.

"Use the light from my lantern to look around. I know it's narrow down there, but I don't think the triplets would put us in this situation without any clues," West says. His tone is soft and reassuring, but he's nervous. I can feel it.

Hannah squints at the walls. "I think there's something written in here. Yes! Hold on." She tilts her head and begins to read aloud. *"You've made it this far, but now you've lost one. Fetch the key that you need to keep having fun."*

I roll off my knees and sit down, then run my fingers over the small lock I can see built into the bars. "The triplets thought this was fun?"

"If we weren't here looking for the treasure and worried about time, I think it would be. These puzzles are cool," West answers.

"Stop chatting and find the key," Hannah growls. "It's cold down here, and you know how I feel about bugs!"

Jumping up, I blink at the shadowy room. There are so many places a key could be hidden. "I hope it isn't under one of the statues."

"Hold up, there's something else." Hannah shifts around in the hole, then gasps. "Yes! I thought I felt something brushing against my hair. There's a piece of metal hanging in here!"

Metal?

"Is it the key?" West asks hopefully. "Never mind. That would be too easy."

"It's not a key. It's shaped like a horseshoe."

Horseshoe-shaped metal.

A memory clicks in my brain. An old cartoon Dad put on

one time to show us what he used to watch as a kid. It was about this cat and mouse who hated each other. The cartoon was terrible, but there was an episode that might help us now...

"I think it's a magnet!" I say, lining my eye up with the opening in the bars so I can see. Hannah gestures to it with her head, and sure enough, I'm right. "That's exactly what it is. Hannah, can you hand it to me?"

"With what?" she asks. "I can't lift my arms."

Uh-oh. She's not going to like what I'm about to suggest. I look at West, who pulls a face. A *glad it's you and not me making this suggestion* face.

I decide to just say it.

"You have to use your nose," I say. "The magnet looks like it's hanging on a nail. Put your nose in the center of the *U* shape, and slowly drag it up to the bars."

"But keep your nose in the middle!" West warns. "Otherwise, it might get unbalanced and fall off."

I blink at him, horrified. Here I thought the worst part about this was Hannah pressing her nose to a dirty old wall covered in spiderwebs. Now I know the worst part is the possibility of her dropping it.

"My *nose*?! Are you guys bananas?"

"No, you're the Banana," West retorts, then holds a hand up as if to say sorry. Definitely not the time for his dad jokes.

I reach two fingers through the bars and touch Hannah's head. "You can do this. You can do anything you set your mind to. You're a Delta."

She sniffs and looks at the magnet, clearly worried.

She's not the only one.

Leaning away from the bars, I shoot a troubled look at West. "What if she drops it off her nose?" I whisper. "What then?"

"We can't think about that. We gotta focus on making sure that doesn't happen." He peers into the hole again, his lips moving like he's counting. "It looks like she needs to drag the magnet about six inches. Then we should be able to reach it."

Hannah nods but stays quiet. I can see her shaking, and it makes me feel terrible. More than anything, I wish I could switch places with her. I'm the one who made us come here, after all.

With a deep breath, Hannah presses her nose to the wall underneath the magnet. She starts moving it upward, quickly lowering it back down onto the nail when it begins to wobble.

"I can't do this. I can't do this."

"Out of the three of us, you are the only one who *can* do it, Hannah. You're coordinated and strong. Every time I went to one of your dance recitals and watched you hold those poses for so long, I was amazed." I wait for her to say something, and when she doesn't, I add: "They were stupid to let you leave. Someday they'll realize that the best student they ever had was a gum-snapping, statue-poking, humming machine named Hannah."

That gets a laugh.

West clears his throat. "We're right here with you. If you fail, we fail. We're a team, Hannah. You're not doing this alone."

With one final breath and a nod, Hannah presses her nose to the wall again and does exactly what I knew she'd do.

Her best.

CHAPTER TWENTY-ONE
JUST LIKE OPERATION

The magnet has moved up an inch. A whopping inch. I'm a nervous wreck, because it's obvious Hannah is terrified of botching this. I would be too.

"You're doing great, Hannah. Just stay steady with it," West says. Then he reaches out and tugs on my sleeve, so I follow him a few feet away. "If something goes wrong, do you want to leave, or do you want me to?"

I'm so confused I don't answer at first. "You mean leave the house? Why would we do that?"

"Because if Hannah drops that magnet, we need to find another way out of this room, or we're in big trouble. She's stuck in there, and we can't even call for help." He shakes his phone at me in case I forgot we don't have a signal.

My mood takes a nosedive. Suddenly I'm not just worried; I'm scared.

"We don't even know *how* to leave the house, West. I'm sure you could remember the directions to get back to the Circus Room, but without the rope, that doesn't help us. The only way out is forward, and even with all three of us working on these riddles, we're barely getting through."

West rubs his face. His eyes are red-rimmed and tired. "Yeah. I don't know if just one of us could make it to the end."

"I wouldn't be able to," I tell him. "Especially not if there are other rooms like this one. This house isn't made for one person to go through at a time."

The odds of Hannah being able to complete this bizarre task start running through my brain. I try to ignore them. I'm learning that sometimes the best way to look at something is the hopeful way—even if it isn't the most practical. Deep down I know there's a good chance Hannah will drop the magnet. Anyone could. But I also know that she needs us right now, and planning for her to fail won't help.

I drop back down to the bars. Hannah has made progress, another inch or so. Unfortunately, she's shaking like a leaf. Nerves and exhaustion are a bad combo.

"Take breaks when you need to. You're so close," I tell her, trying to sound positive. It's a good thing she can't see me very well. Beads of sweat are building on my forehead, and I can't stop shaking.

"I'm not close at all," she responds through gritted teeth. "The magnet keeps slipping off my nose."

Maybe what we need here is a distraction. Something to take Hannah's mind off how hard this is. "Remember last summer when I found that old game in a box at my house? *Operation*?"

West raises his hand. "I remember! That stupid buzzer went off every time I touched the tweezers. I swear, that game hated me."

I laugh at the memory. West had gotten so frustrated that he quit. His face was red, his hands were clenched, and I ended up closing my bedroom window to make sure he couldn't throw the game out of it.

"Hannah, you rocked that game. It was like you were meant for it. This isn't much different. You have to be slow and steady to win." I stop talking, hoping that I'm being a good friend. Hannah came here for me. She showed up for me. Now I need to show up for her.

With a soft groan, Hannah pushes the magnet up again. It wobbles on the top of her nose, and she stops moving to reposition. When she starts up again, I snap at West to get closer.

"It's almost up here. Do you want to grab it, or should I?" I ask him.

He laughs. "I have sausage fingers. You do it. Yours will fit through the bars better."

Maybe West has forgotten that I wasn't that good at *Operation* either. I wiggle my fingers, my heart thudding uncomfortably.

"Is it close? Is it close enough?" Hannah asks.

"I think so. Don't move." I slowly stick my index finger through the slats. I can't reach the magnet. "Just another little bit, Hannah."

She whimpers but ever so slowly starts moving the magnet again. When it bumps my finger, I tell her to stop.

"I'm going to try to pull it up, but don't move your nose, okay?"

West points at a spot in the bars. "That looks wider to me. Try there. You might be able to get two fingers through instead of just the one."

He's right. I angle differently and stick my pointer and middle finger through. Then I position them on either side of the magnet and start pinching it upward. It's awkward and slow, but it's working. Hannah rises onto her tiptoes to follow the magnet with her nose.

When I get it to the top, I hold it still while West grabs it.

He stands up, holding the magnet over his head like a trophy. His whoop is so loud it doesn't even sound like him.

Hannah blinks up through the bars. The tip of her nose is completely black, and her eyes are watering. "Oh my god. We did it. I can't believe we did it."

"No," I start, "*you* did it."

She smiles through her fatigue. Even though I originally wished I could trade places with her, I'm actually really glad Hannah got that experience. Maybe now she'll finally believe in herself again.

"I'm going to help West figure out what we need to do with the magnet, okay? Will you be okay alone for a few minutes?"

"Yes," she says, a shiver rolling through her. "Just get me out of here. Please?"

I stand up and find West. He's examining the magnet and mumbling.

"This can't be very strong," he tells me, lifting it up and down as if trying to estimate the weight. "I mean, I'm not a magnet expert, but it seems light."

"Do you think it's fake?" I ask. "Not everything in escape rooms is real or even means anything."

West grimaces. "If it is fake, I'm not telling Hannah. We just put her through a ton of stress, and it better not have been for nothing."

No kidding. If the magnet isn't real, I'm officially going to find the triplets' graves and give them a piece of my mind.

"Guess we won't know unless we test it though." West sets his lantern down and places the magnet near the metal handle. It jumps up slightly before flopping back down. "It's real. I can feel the magnet working."

Whew. "What did the riddle say again? We need to find the key?"

"*Fetch*. It said we need to 'fetch' the key," West corrects. "That wording makes me think this isn't going to be easy. And I'm guessing we'll need this." He holds the magnet up in the air between us.

Out of all the escape rooms we've done, I only remember one that involved a magnet. We had to place specific objects on a magnetized table to make a secret passage open. This magnet doesn't seem like it's made for that.

"Ticktock, people!" Hannah calls out.

"We're trying!" I shout back. My eyes find West. I don't want to say it out loud because I don't want Hannah to overhear, but I'm still scared. It's good that we found the magnet. Definitely a step in the right direction. Still, my stomach feels like it's eating itself, and I'm thirsty now too. Add in the fact that I have to pee, and this is becoming a nightmare. What if we end up here overnight. Or longer?

West looks back at me. His cheek is smudged with dirt, and his hair still has flecks of rainbow-colored confetti in it. But those aren't the things that catch my eye the most. It's his expression. West has a lot of different serious expressions, but this one is the most serious of all. It's also the most frightening.

He's scared too.

"We can do this," I say. "Right?"

"We have to."

I take a deep breath in through my nose and blow it out from my mouth. Then I do it again. How long we've been in the funhouse doesn't matter anymore. All that matters in this moment is that we get Hannah out of the hole. I want the treasure; I really do. But I also want my friends to be safe.

It would also be great if I don't pee my pants, but I guess beggars can't be choosers.

CHAPTER TWENTY-TWO

A GRATE DISCOVERY

West and I decide to start by examining the statues one by one. Since there isn't any furniture in the room, and no bookshelves or obvious trapdoors, there isn't much choice.

"I don't know what I'm looking for," West says.

"Just anything that sticks out." I move from statue to statue, my heart quickening. I know I'm rushing too much, but I can't help it. The pressure of having a best friend trapped in the floor and our time running out is getting to me.

Slow down, just slow down, I say to myself. *You're playing sloppy and you're going to miss something.*

I move on to the next statue and freeze.

"Something wrong?" West asks.

"No. I mean, I don't know. This one looks familiar." I look

it up and down, trying to figure out why I feel like I've seen it before. Glasses. Stoic expression. A suit with buttons. That's when I remember. There's another one exactly like it on the other side of the room. I noticed it when I walked over to see the dog sculpture West busted. "I think there are two of these."

I lead West to the other side and show him the statue. Sure enough, they're identical.

His eyes widen. "There's a third one. I didn't think about it until you showed me these two, but there's another one with glasses right next to the door we climbed through. I remember thinking it seemed like he was greeting me."

West jogs over to the third statue and points. "It's the same, right?"

Identical. Even the clothing is the same.

Their clothing is the same.

"West," I breathe out. "I think these are the triplets."

I jog back and forth between the three statues a few times, making sure they're the same. They are, down to the little round glasses perched on their stony noses. "Remember the picture we found of them when we were researching? This is them."

West looks impressed. "I do! And yeah, I think you're right."

Even though I'm happy for this little breakthrough, I still feel a *teeny* bit weird about all the research we did. In a normal escape room, I'd consider that cheating. I never look up anything about it beforehand. Neither do West and Hannah. But this place is different. It's a funhouse. It's also old and the stakes are so, so high. The future of my family is much more important than an ugly T-shirt and bragging rights.

"Did you guys find something?" Hannah calls out.

"Yes!" I yell back. "Three of these statues are the triplets!"

"What does that mean?" she asks.

I exchange a look with West. "Um, well, we aren't sure yet. But something!"

Hannah groans again.

"Oh, wait. They *aren't* identical," West says. He's holding his lantern up to the face of one of the statues. "At least their expressions aren't. Their eyes are pointing different directions, see? This one is looking to the right, but the one across the room has eyes that are looking to the left."

"And this one"—I tap on the third triplet—"is looking straight ahead."

"That means they're all looking..." he starts, following the line of their eyesight with his index finger. "Right there."

I blink at the spot West is pointing at. It's just an empty stretch of wall. At least it looks like that. "We must've missed something over there. Maybe another hidden door?"

"A kitten snore?" Hannah shouts. "What does that mean?"

"No! A *hidden door*!" I say, laughing.

"Talk louder! I can't hear anything down here!"

Apparently.

West begins knocking on the wall like he always does. Up and down. Down and up. Time to bring back the pattern. I walk to the other end of the wall so I can help him. Knocking down by the floorboards, I slowly work my way up as far as I can reach. When West and meet in the middle of the wall at the two wooden doors, his expression is pure frustration.

"Every knock sounds the same. And I don't see hinges or cracks in the wall that could be a sign of a hidden door. We only have the two obvious wooden doors." He exhales loudly and looks over at the place where Hannah's pedestal sank. "We gotta move faster, Sarah. She's brave, but this is a lot."

"I know. I just feel lost." I'm just about to go recheck the eyes of the triplet statues to make sure we didn't search the wrong area when I notice something. A grate set into the floor. "What is that?"

West cocks an eyebrow. "It *could* be nothing."

I cock an eyebrow back. "Or it could be *everything*."

We drop down onto our hands and knees. The grate is about the same length as the registers in our house that blow out cold air in the summer and warm air in the winter. But this grate is fancier. Gold with a symbol engraved into it.

A deck of cards!

"West," I say. Adrenaline floods me.

"I see it! Must mean we're on the right track." West immediately sets his lantern over the grate, thumping on the lantern when the flickering starts up again. "Do you see anything else?"

Putting my face down so close to the grate that my nose touches it, I look in. Lying in the bottom of the shallow rectangle is a dust-covered key. I sit upright, practically shaking with excitement. "It's down there. A key is down there!"

"Since the door doesn't have a lock on it, that has to be for Hannah's cage," West says. "We found the key, Hannah! We're coming!"

We look back and forth between the key and the magnet in his hand. Apparently, we're supposed to pull the key up out of the grate using the magnet. He holds it out to me. "You were always better at *Operation*."

I laugh and snatch it from him; then I get to work.

A few ragged breaths later, West and I are racing back to Hannah's hole in the floor with the key in our hands. I dropped it more than once while trying to maneuver it out of the grate, but considering how nervous I was, I'm happy. We still don't know how to get out of this room, but at least we can free her.

"We're totally playing *Operation* again when we get out of here," I tell him.

"You go right ahead," he says, chuckling. "I still hear that buzzer in my sleep."

"You got it?" Hannah asks as we draw close, another huge shiver racking her body. She cranes her neck up to look at us through the bars. "Please say yes. Something crawled over my hand a minute ago, and I don't even want to think about what it was."

"We got it," I say, inserting the key into the lock. Turning it, I breathe a sigh of relief when the bars loosen. I grip them with both hands and slide them open. "Help me grab her, West. She can't use her arms, so we'll have to pull her out."

West gets down on his knees. "I'll take her left side, and you take the right. If we pull up from her armpits, I think we can do this."

Hannah groans. "First bugs, then this. I swear, the triplets hated me, and we never even met."

"The triplets didn't hate you. They just wanted to make their funhouse extra interesting," West says. "It's my fault you're down there to begin with. I broke the dog."

"It's no one's fault," I interrupt. "But really, we're lucky Hannah ended up down there."

Hannah looks up at me through the bars, her mouth gaping. "Um, how do you figure?"

"Because if we used the dog statue instead, we wouldn't have seen the clue written on the inside of the pedestal wall until much later. We also would've had to find a different way to get the magnet out, and who knows how long that could have taken."

Hannah tries to hide her smile and fails. "So my nose saved the day?"

West laughs. It's loud and echoes off the walls, making me laugh too. "Yup. Your nose saved the day. Instead of Banana, I'll just call you Nostrils from now on. That good?"

A snort-laugh escapes Hannah. "No, thank you. I'll stick with being a fruit, thank you very much."

Waving my hand around in a circular motion, I try to get my friends' attention. "Love this little bonding moment you guys are having, but we gotta move. Are you ready, West?"

West sticks his hands down into the cylinder and nods. "Ready as I'll ever be."

"All right, here we go. On the count of three." I slide my hands under Hannah's arm. "One...two...three!"

Grunting, West and I pull up on Hannah as hard as possible. She slides upward far enough to use her arms to help push herself up and out the rest of the way.

I don't waste any time in hugging her. Her skin is cold and dirty, and I know how frightened she was down there.

The three pedestals we stood on begin rising back into their original places. When they reach their full height, there's a click.

Then two epically huge things happen...

The wooden doors pop open.

And a lantern goes out.

CHAPTER TWENTY-THREE
A GLOWING BOOTY

"We're down to one lantern," I say, the adrenaline wearing off. "That's going to make this hard."

Hannah is still brushing the dirt from her clothes. Even though she's rubbed at her nose since she got out of the cylinder, it's still darker than the rest of her skin. She looks like she started painting her face for Halloween but quit.

West hits the side of the dead lantern a few times, then reluctantly tucks it into his backpack. "I should've brought batteries."

"You brought the lanterns. Neither of us thought to do that," Hannah says. "Maybe the next room will be brighter."

At first Hannah's comment seems silly. Every room here has been dark, so dark we can barely see our hands in front of our faces without the lanterns on. But now I realize there's a reason, besides the very big reason that there's no electricity. "All the windows have been boarded up, but maybe there's a way to uncover the one in the next room?"

West laughs. It's one of his *I can't believe this* laughs though.

"What? Do you think that's a stupid idea?" I ask, tapping my foot on the ground.

"Not at all. I think it's stupid that we didn't think of that before now. I was so focused on the challenges that I didn't even notice the windows. How many rooms have we done in the dark? Four?" He shakes his head. "Based on the fact that a statue or human could lower the pedestal Hannah got stuck in, I'm pretty sure there was more than one way to complete each room we've done. I wonder how many clues we missed because we didn't have enough light."

Hannah puts a fresh piece of gum in her mouth, then frowns at the empty package. "That just makes us even more amazing. We're beating their house and doing it in the dark!"

Hannah's optimism is contagious. I nod along with her. "She's right. Don't look back." I put my hand on the wooden door. It's open a crack, not enough to see into the next room, but enough to notice that something is different. A sliver of light is cutting through the darkness. "Looks like we aren't going to have to worry about the dead lantern anyway."

I tap my toe on the small beam of light on the floor.

"And let's not forget, this could be the last room," Hannah says. She's rubbing her hands together as she says this. I'm sure it's to warm up, but it makes her look like she's plotting something evil. "For all we know, those wooden doors lead straight to the treasure! Maybe the light is from the piles and piles of gold."

The idea of being so close to the treasure makes my mouth go dry. I clap my hands together, startling West. "I'm going. Light or no light, I want to finish this thing."

I put both palms flat on the wooden doors. Then I send a big wish out into the universe: *Let this be the treasure. Please.*

The doors open and I'm instantly blinded. I put an arm up over my eyes.

"I knew it! It's the glow of booty!" Hannah screams. She's plowing past me, her dust-covered hair trailing her like she's some sort of wacky Rapunzel.

I'm laughing so hard that I couldn't open my eyes if I wanted to. Hannah using the word *booty* to describe whatever treasure she's imagining is hilarious.

Uncovering my eyes, I realize Hannah was wrong. There is no gold. There isn't even a treasure. There's just a window that's missing part of a board. Sunlight is streaming in, reflecting off every surface and making the room look golden.

And stunning.

At first, I'm too shocked to speak. The room we're standing

in is nothing like I expected. There are no boxes hanging from the ceiling, no bookshelves lining the walls, and no Roman sculptures perched on pedestals. Instead, there are mirrors. A long mirrored hallway stretches out in front of us. Our reflection stares back at us from the end of it. I wince at our tired, ragged appearances. I thought I looked bad in the Box Room, but that was nothing compared to this. Someone could hang me out in a field as a scarecrow at this point.

"I thought there weren't any mirror mazes in here. Isn't this a little lame for the triplets?" I ask.

"No way it's going to be lame. Nothing they've done so far in this house is basic." West takes a step into the mirrored hall and points up. "Check it out. It's like a corn maze, only with mirrors. See how there's no ceiling? This is just one big room. They separated it into smaller spaces using partitions to make it into a mirror maze."

Just one glimpse of the maze sprawled out ahead of us is enough to transform Hannah's expression. Instead of being filled with curiosity like it normally is, it's obvious that she's dreading this. She absentmindedly rubs her nose, a reminder of the last time the Deltas took on a mirror maze.

"This won't be like last time," I reassure her.

"And how do you know that? My nose has already been through a lot today!"

"Because we learned from our mistakes. No running in this one." I pause and look down the hall, nerves flooding me. "And no getting separated."

West draws in a deep breath and puts a hand on her shoulder. "We were being stupid that day, Hannah. It wasn't even an escape room. Just us running around a mirror maze at a dumb carnival."

Hannah nods, but I see uncertainty in her eyes. The last, and only, time we attempted a mirror maze, Hannah got overexcited and ran in a different direction than West and me. At one point, there was a giant *thunk*, and she started screaming. By the time West and I found her, she was on the floor holding her *very* broken nose. Apparently, she saw a reflection of West and ran toward it, thinking it was him.

It wasn't. Lesson learned. Never trust anything in a mirror maze.

Also, never trust the triplets.

My eyes glide up past the top of the hallway to the only gap in the mirrors—the windows. Even though one is still fully covered, I recognize the shapes from when we first arrived at the house. The oval window and the skinny rectangular window.

We've just taken our first steps into the hallway when a familiar sound stops us.

A phone ding.

CHAPTER TWENTY-FOUR
THE DING HEARD ROUND
THE WORLD

"Whose phone was that?" I ask, hastily rummaging around in my pocket for mine. I check the screen, but it looks the same as it has since we got in. No bars. No signal at all. "It wasn't mine."

"Not mine either," West holds his up.

Hannah is staring at her phone, her face quickly draining of what little color it had. "It...it was mine."

"You have a signal?" I ask, crowding around her side to see her screen.

"I guess I did for a minute. Must've been a spot we passed or something. It's gone now though, but..." She trails off, her mouth turned down into a frown. "Oh...oh no."

"Hannah, what is it? Was it your parents? What did they say?" West is firing off questions so fast I can barely follow him.

"It was." She looks up, her eyes swimming with tears. "I looked up some news articles about this place before I left. Just wanted to see how many rooms there are."

"And?" I prompt.

"Sixteen. But you don't have to do all of them to escape."

"Not that, Hannah!" I snap, annoyed. "I mean, why do the articles you looked up matter?"

"Oh. That. Well, apparently my parents tried to call me because they need me home sooner, and when they couldn't reach me, they tried to use my laptop to ping my phone. The articles were all up on the screen in different tabs." Fresh tears spill over and run down her cheeks.

The world starts spinning. I look from West to Hannah. "Are you saying they know where we are?"

"Yes," she croaks out. "They know *exactly* where we are."

I never understood the phrase, "Time stood still," until just now. "When was that text sent?"

Hannah shrugs. "There's no way to know. It came in just now, but it could have been sent anytime. What if they sent it an hour ago when we didn't have any signal?"

"And you're sure you don't have signal now?" West says.

"Go back outside the hall and see if you can find it. If you can get a text them fast enough, maybe they won't come here."

She does what he asks, holding her phone up in the air every which direction trying to find a bar. After a minute, she gives up and squats down on the floor, her face covered with her hands. "We're in so much trouble, guys. What if they have your parents with them? My mom knows your moms. She could have told them."

West looks so defeated it's scary.

I start running probabilities in my head. Of course, her mother probably called mine, maybe even West's too. She's very protective of Hannah, so once she found out her daughter isn't where she's supposed to be, she would've been scared. My mom is at work today. If she had to leave unexpectedly, she could get in trouble or, worse, lose her job. And even worse than all that, if they decide to come here, we could have to kiss our shot at finding the treasure goodbye. This will all have been for nothing, absolutely nothing.

"What do we do?" Hannah sniffs.

"We move fast," I say, tugging her back into the mirrored hallway with West and me. "We might have five minutes before they show up; we might have fifty. This is obviously not the best situation. But it's not the end for us. Not yet. Even if our parents all show up, how will they get to us in here?"

West tilts his head to the side, a tiny smile playing on his lips. "They'd have to go through the funhouse. It will take them time, maybe a lot of time. I've seen my parents try an escape room, and it wasn't pretty." He reaches into his pocket and holds out the keys we've collected so far. "Plus, without these it's going to be tough."

"West!" I throw my arms around him. He stiffens for a moment, then pulls back with a full goofy grin. "I'm so happy you remembered to keep those safe!"

"Of course, I did," he says, laughing. "It's impossible not to, remember?"

I smile back, my heart warming with the idea that for once, West isn't embarrassed by his gift. He looks proud.

"You guys really think we can still do this?" Hannah asks. Her face is dry now, but her lip is still quivering. "I'm just so sorry I messed everything up."

"Don't be. We've all screwed up," I say, gesturing for her and West to keep moving. I hate rushing but there's no choice. "You didn't expect them to get into your laptop. Which, by the way, you *clearly* need to change your password for."

Hannah snorts, then bursts into laughter. "Ya think? Apparently, it wasn't hard to guess my password." She pauses for a moment, looking sheepish. "ILOVEGUM."

West laughs so hard he's running a palm over the

mirrors to look for clues with one hand and clutching his stomach with the other. I put one of my own hands on the chilly glass and let myself enjoy the moment. Even though it isn't perfect, nothing ever is. There are parents—probably angry ones—headed here, and who knows how we'll be punished for this. Still, I'm happy. Out of all the escape rooms we've done together, this is my favorite. I never realized how much I trust West and Hannah until now, and based on the secrets they've both shared today, I'm not sure they did either. It makes me even more determined to find this treasure. I can't move to Michigan.

"Hey, keep your hands out in front of you," Hannah reminds us. "I learned the hard way that if you don't do that, you're cruisin' for a bruisin'."

Despite my anxiety, I giggle.

Suddenly the hall dead-ends with two different routes available. Left or right.

"Uh-oh. Which way?" West asks.

I look down one hall, then the other. They seem identical. Pretty much my worst nightmare. Without any difference in the two halls, how are we supposed to know which way is correct? At least the rest of the house had symbols and hints.

"Sarah?" West says, jostling me. "You with us?"

Nodding, I take one more look both ways. "Yeah. I'm

just not sure. I hate that there's no way to tell which path is correct. Maybe they both hold a clue, but most of the time, that's not true."

"Just pick," Hannah says. "Like you said, we gotta move fast."

My brain goes haywire. Two paths. Only one is correct. That means we have a fifty-fifty shot at being right, no matter which way we pick. Those are the same odds we had back in the Box Room when we had to choose that final box. And we picked wrong.

"The buzzer is close, Sarah," West says. "If you don't pick a route soon, we'll lose no matter what."

He's absolutely right. With tests, you're never supposed to leave a question unanswered. It's better to guess and at least have a chance of getting it correct. This is the same. Picking one of these two routes might keep us in the game. Without thinking I swerve left, feeling sick to my stomach.

Holding my hands out front, I follow the walls around corner after corner. There's no sign of anything. No end, no hints, no boxes, or clues. Nothing. We make a final turn, and I gasp as my hands meet the mirror more forcefully than they have before. It's the wall.

We hit a dead end.

CHAPTER TWENTY-FIVE
MAKE YOUR MARK

Turning back the opposite direction, I think about the first mirror maze we did. The only way we found our way out after Hannah hurt her nose was to look for familiar marks on the glass. West and I both noticed full-sized handprints on some of the mirrors at one juncture on our way in, so when we saw those again, we knew we were close. Problem is, this mirror maze doesn't have any markings because we're the first people in it.

We'll have to make them ourselves.

I slow to a stop and tug on Hannah's bag.

"Hey," she says, stumbling backward. "You trying to give me another broken nose?"

"No, I'm trying to get out your lip gloss."

Hannah looks puzzled but unzips her backpack and hands it to me. I hold it up, noticing that although it's mostly clear, there's just enough of a red tinge to work. Moving forward, I stop at the T intersection where we turned left before and use the lip gloss applicator to make an X on the mirror.

"Ohhh, you're marking the spot! Like bread crumbs," West says.

"Exactly," I say, moving into the other path. "If we come across this X again, we'll know not to go that way. That it's a dead end."

"And my mom said that lip gloss was a waste of money," Hannah says, looking smug.

"Don't mention your mom," West says, scowling. "All it does is remind me that she's on her way, probably with a bunch of police officers and maybe even some of those scary German shepherds."

Hannah's jaw drops. "German shepherds are not scary! They're adorable."

"We'll see if you think they're adorable when one is eating your arm," West says with a snort. "That's probably why no one has seen or heard from William Taters since he tried to break in."

"Dogs did not chew up William Taters." I say, keeping my hands out in front as we continue down the new path. Like the first one, it's confusing. With so many turns and nothing but our reflections surrounding us, it's hard to tell what's real and what's not. "He probably just decided to stay off the radar after being caught breaking in."

"Off the radar, huh?" West says. "That's just code for *busy sewing one of the armholes in all of his shirts closed.*"

"He's not missing an arm!" I snap, then skid to a stop as we round the corner. There's a box on the floor. It's shaped like a miniature pirate chest.

Hannah rushes over to it. "I don't see a lock."

"Open it," West and I say in unison. Is it risky? Maybe. But there isn't time to be safe. The parents could be really close by now. For all we know, they're outside already, trying to figure out how to get in.

She cracks the lid of the box open, revealing a piece of paper. Unfolding it, Hannah begins reading, "*The moment you seek is close at hand; this house is almost done. Use the thing you shouldn't waste to make sure that it's won.*"

"Use the thing you shouldn't waste," West repeats. "Toilet paper?"

Hannah slaps a hand over her mouth.

"What?" West says. "Am I the only one who remembers how it all just disappeared during the pandemic?"

"I remember," I start, taking the paper from Hannah so

I can read it myself. I flip it over to look for any other clues. "But I don't think that's the answer to this riddle. Where are we going to get toilet paper?"

"Right. It's gotta be something that everyone has, or the triplets would have to give it to us in the maze," Hannah adds. "Like they gave us the rope in the Circus Room. And since I haven't seen any toilet paper hanging around..."

West rubs at his jaw. "Okay, so that's not it. What's something we all have that we wouldn't want to waste?"

Glancing at her lip gloss in my hand, Hannah says, "Well, it can't be something like makeup. Not everyone uses that."

West nods. "Could it be money?"

I let out a half laugh. "I'm proof that can't be it because I don't have any. You guys had to buy my train ticket for today, remember?"

Hannah dangles her house keys. "Everyone has keys to *something*, right?"

"Do they? What about homeless people? They wouldn't have a house or a car," I argue.

West nods in agreement. "And how would you 'waste' keys? Even if everyone did have keys, it doesn't make sense with that part of the riddle."

Dropping them back into her bag, Hannah groans. "Wrappers, wallet, headphones. Ugh. I don't think there's even one thing in my bag that everyone would have. And there's no way there is anything that works in your bag, West. You've probably got some really weird stuff in there."

West's eyebrows scrunch up. "I have totally normal things in my bag! You're the one with a hundred sticks of gum!"

It's a good thing I've gotten used to their bickering, because I can think through it now. I keep repeating the riddle in my head, stalling on the word *waste*. I could be wrong, but it seems like the key to this whole thing.

There are a lot of things we don't waste now that Dad isn't working. Food. Money. Time. I stand up straighter.

"Time! Could it be time?"

Yes. That has to be it.

Most modern escape rooms have a timer. Maybe this funhouse was going to also.

West's eyes travel upward as if he's considering. "Maybe. But the riddle is supposed to help us figure out which way to go? We already know we have to hurry, so I don't know if *time* really works."

I don't how to respond to that. *Time* seemed so perfect, but West is right, it doesn't really feel like a clue.

Just when I think the answer will never come to us, West and Hannah start arguing again.

"I have *practical* things in here, Banana. The lanterns were in this bag, remember?"

Hannah scoffs. "What else is in there though? Bet you have a shoehorn or a shark tooth or some other stupid thing." West opens his mouth to argue, but she holds up her hand. "Don't waste your breath. You've already lost this one, buddy."

West and I both freeze.

Hannah blinks at us like we're aliens from outer space. "What is wrong with you guys?"

I shake her, my excitement too much to control. "Breath! Hannah, do you even hear yourself?"

She thinks back through what she said, a smile slowly spreading across her face. "Everyone has breath."

"And breath fogs up glass," West adds.

"And fogged-up glass could reveal secret messages," I finish.

And just like that, the three of us start panting on the mirrors like we just ran a marathon.

CHAPTER TWENTY-SIX

HOT GARBAGE

West is the first one to find a hint. He stops breathing, stares at the mirror, then breathes on it again. "*The path you seek is straight ahead. Do not lose sight or you'll be...*" He stops reading.

"Be what? West, finish!" I snap.

"*Dead*," he says, looking up at me. "That's scary."

"I don't like it," Hannah says, shuddering.

Me either, but like the riddle said, forward is our only option. Besides, this is a funhouse. The triplets wouldn't have created a room that would hurt the people going through it on purpose.

Right?

"Let's keep going, but carefully," West suggests. "And

don't stop breathing on the mirrors. We don't want to miss any clues."

Hannah wrinkles her nose up.

"What now?" I ask.

"Nothing. Just that one of you has breath like hot garbage."

A laugh sputters out of me. "Well maybe you should share your gum more often!"

Suddenly, I notice West's rhythmic breathing has stopped. He's slumped against the mirror, his head drooping down.

"West? Are you okay?" I shake his shoulder.

He waves me off. "I'm fine. Just a little light-headed is all. Probably from all the heavy breathing."

"Oh! I've heard of that! It happens to people when they blow up a lot of balloons too." Hannah puts a finger on her chin. "What's it called?"

"Hyperventilating," West answers. He pulls himself more upright, but his face is pale. "This is bad. It's slowing us down."

Hannah pulls a tie from the front of her bag then sweeps her hair up into a ponytail. "Maybe that's what they wanted. If the funhouse was going to have a buzzer or maybe even a prize for people who completed it quickly, this could be one of the ways the triplets slowed people down."

"Diabolical," West pants. "We're so close to the end, and the thing slowing us down is...us!"

"You don't look as pale now though. That's good."

His frog tongue is sticking out again too. Always a good sign.

When West feels like moving again, we continue. Breathing on the mirrors hard enough and long enough to reveal clues is hard work, and before I know it, I'm feeling light-headed too.

I call out for Hannah to slow down, but she's already stopped. Blinking through the spots fading in and out of my eyesight, I see that she's frantically feeling around the mirrors with both hands.

"What's wrong?" I ask.

"It's a dead end. The hall... It just ends here."

"That's not possible," West grumbles. "The clue clearly said that the path we seek is straight ahead. We haven't turned at all, right?"

I don't think we've turned, but with light glinting off every surface and bits and pieces of our own reflections jumping around, it's hard to know for sure.

"Wait!" Hannah yells. She's crouched down near the floor. "There's an opening here. It's small, but I think we can crawl through."

Oh goody. Another tight space.

Hannah gets down on her hands and knees and scurries through. I follow, then West. We end up in a room that takes my breath away. Triangular mirrors cover the walls in a pattern that makes the room appear to stretch on forever. I take another step in, mesmerized by the illusion.

"Equilateral triangles," West says. "They used them to create this effect."

More triangles. Maybe I was wrong about signs, and they do exist.

"It looks like it never ends, like it just goes on and on to infinity." Hannah takes a few steps in, stumbling forward when the flooring suddenly changes. "What the heck?"

I pull my eyes away from the geometric patterns that make up the walls and look down. The floor where Hannah stumbled is strange, sunken in an irregular shape. Kind of like a misshapen circle or the outline of a pond.

"What do you think this was supposed to be?" I say, bending down to touch the floor surface. It's rough, like sandpaper.

West is scratching his head. "No clue. It almost looks like it was going to be a really shallow pool."

I let out a guffaw. Based on how it looks, what West is saying makes sense. But it doesn't make sense inside a funhouse. "They wouldn't put a pool in a mirror maze."

"But we didn't think they'd put a trapeze in here either, and they did," Hannah points out.

True. The triplets were a lot of things—odd, determined, resilient—but they weren't predictable. I pace the inside of the sunken area, my brain caught on whether it's important. Every escape room has distractions. Maybe this is one of them.

"I think we should keep moving. This just looks like another half-finished part of the funhouse to me."

"Same," West says. He walks up a short ramp leading out of the pool-like area and...

CLICK.

"What was that?" Hannah asks nervously. "Because it sounded like a—"

"Button," I finish for her, panic rising in me. A grinding sound starts up from somewhere in the room. I spin in a circle, disoriented.

West lifts his foot and looks beneath it. Sure enough, there's another hidden button. "Sorry, guys. It blends in really well, and I just didn't see it."

"Did the walls move?" I ask. "Tell me the walls didn't move."

As if the room itself decides to answer my question, three sections of mirror begin to reposition themselves. They slide backward into the walls, creating three new doorways. A rolled-up piece of paper drops from a hole in the ceiling.

Hannah looks unsettled. She crouches down and picks up the note. It's another scroll, this time tied up in green ribbon. She unties it, then holds the scroll out for us to see the emblem printed on it.

The wishbone.

My stomach lurches.

"Can you read it, Hannah? Out loud?" West asks.

Hannah nods gravely. "*Dead in the water, but not for long. Guess which door is right and which two are wrong.*"

Dead in the water. I look back at the sunken area of the room. Maybe a pool does make sense in a mirror maze, after all. I think back to all my Dad's funny sayings over the years... sayings that made no sense if you didn't already know what they meant.

That guy has a chip on his shoulder.

Don't beat around the bush.

Those are a dime a dozen.

Looks like we're dead in the water.

The last one raises goose bumps on my arms. Dad said that exact same thing when Mom finally showed him the foreclosure notice. I'd been standing outside their bedroom door, listening in.

"West was right. This was going to be filled with water. Think about it—the second half of that clue said that if we didn't stay straight, we'd be dead." I gesture at the pool area. "It's another play on words. *Dead in the water*."

"I've never heard that saying," West says.

"I have," Hannah says gravely. "It means we failed."

CHAPTER TWENTY-SEVEN
LOTTERY TICKETS SUCK

We failed. The words rattle around in my head like loose screws. Only moments ago, this mirror maze was mesmerizing. Now it feels like a nightmare.

West kicks at nothing. His face is red as he looks at the three new exits. "This has to be a joke."

If only it were a joke. Instead, I have the feeling it's another punishment. We probably made a mistake somewhere, and the triplets created this little side challenge to make things harder, just like they did with the duplicate Box Room. I replay the hints we found on the mirrors in my mind. The last one very clearly said to stay straight.

"Guys. When we got to the spot where Hannah said the hallway ended, we turned. Remember? The small passageway we crawled through to get in here was to our right." I shake my head. Such a rookie mistake.

Hannah looks at me incredulously. "What else were we supposed to do? The hallway *ended*."

"I bet it didn't. We just rushed when you found the opening to this room and took it. There was probably a hidden door that went straight." West sighs and rubs his eyes. "If we'd just taken our time instead of rushing..."

"No one would figure that out!" Hannah exclaims. Her hair is falling out of the ponytail again, strands of it falling down her back and around her face. "We're never going to make it now. Not with the parents on the way."

Her souring mood scares me. Dad always says that giving up can become a habit. Once you do it, it's easier to do again and again. Maybe that happened with Hannah when she quit dance. I don't know for sure, but I do know that if she wants to quit trying in this funhouse, I'm not going to make it easy for her. Good friends encourage each other.

"No," I say, then again more firmly. "No!"

Hannah and West stop pacing to look at me.

"We did not come this far to be stopped by a mirror maze." I look at the three doors, anger building in me. "We did all the hard rooms. We finished them when no one else could. We can handle this one too. This isn't the end."

I let out my frustration in an extralong sigh.

"We need to finish strong. I just don't know how," I gesture at the doors. "You heard that clue. There's no strategy to this room at all."

I rack my brain to make sense of the clue. Why would the triplets leave such an important challenge up to luck? Everything else has been so carefully planned. Even the books in the library weren't disorganized, even though they appeared to be. Perhaps that means this room is intentional too.

"Guys. What if no strategy *was* their strategy?" I ask. "Think about it—every room in this funhouse has tested us somehow! Hannah had to learn to be patient. West had to finally accept and use his good memory."

"Omagosh. This could be your test," Hannah whispers. "You *hate* taking risks. More than I hate running out of gum!"

"How is that possible though?" West asks. "The triplets didn't know us. They didn't know Sarah. How could they create this final room to test her specifically?"

The article about them surfaces in my brain. Parents died in a car crash. In orphanages at eight. Separated until in their twenties.

"They didn't need to know me," I say quietly. "They learned the hard way that sometimes you can't control or predict things. Life is...challenging."

"So there's no choice," West says. "We pick a door and deal with the consequences."

"Exactly. It's all luck now. Dumb luck, but that's what they wanted it to be." I slide down the wall until I'm sitting and let my body fold in on itself. "I hate this so much."

Suddenly, I feel warmth on either side of me. Hannah and West. Their shoulders brush mine as they sit down, a reminder that even though I feel alone, I'm not.

"Look, I know you like to control things. You like to run numbers and figure out odds. But it's not always possible. Sometimes life just doesn't give us the chance to plan, you know?" West pauses and looks me straight in the eyes. Suddenly I get the feeling he isn't just talking about the mirror maze. He's talking about my dad too.

"Things happen," he continues. "Stuff goes wrong. We just gotta roll with it and do our best."

"I'm trying," I whimper. "So hard. I just want things to be normal again."

I want Sean to be able to pick a college because he *wants* to go there and not because he thinks it's the only thing we can afford. I want to take long family walks on Sunday mornings again. I want people to look at me without pity in their eyes, and Mom to only work one job. I want Dad to be around again.

West drapes an arm around my shoulders. "I want that too, but I think we have to accept that it might not happen."

Squeezing my eyes shut, I nod. When the doctors first diagnosed Dad, they said even though he'd always have CFS, he could still have good days. Days when he felt like hanging out with us, or helping Mom cook dinner or do laundry. Even when I do everything I can to make those things happen, sometimes it just isn't enough. I guess West is right. I can't control life no matter how much I want to.

Maybe I need to accept that I can't control this mirror maze either.

The idea is terrifying.

I look around at the reflection staring back at me from a thousand different angles. I'm not a quitter, but the girl in the mirror looks like she is. Her face is drawn and streaked with tears, and her body is curled up like a roly-poly. Yet this is the same girl who faced her fear of heights on a trapeze earlier today. And who barreled down a dark slide when she thought her friends were in danger. And who snuck out of the city for just the tiniest chance of saving her family. And who is about to pee in a dank, scary corner if we don't get out soon.

If I'm strong enough to face all that, then I'm strong enough to face this room.

Standing up, I shake off the bad feelings swirling around in me. "I'm sorry."

"For having a moment?" Hannah says, laughing. "If we're apologizing for stuff like that, then I need to get started because I have a *lot* of moments."

This gets a laugh out of me. West too.

"No. I'm sorry that I got so wound up about the stuff I can't control that I forgot about the stuff I *can* control," I tell her. "Like my attitude. I told you we weren't giving up, and I meant it."

West and Hannah open their mouths to say something, but I hold a hand up. "I know. I know. Deltas never give up."

Hannah is the first to stick her fist out. West does the same, gently bumping his knuckles against hers. Then it's my turn. I put my fist out like I'm an athlete and my team is about to break before a big game. Because that's what this is...a big, *big* game. The triplets wanted their funhouse to be challenging. They wanted it to be the most interesting one that ever existed, and so far, they've succeeded.

It's time for the Deltas to succeed now too. Luck or no luck, I'm not quitting.

Taking a deep breath, I point at the last opening in the wall. The third exit.

"Three is our magic number. Let's do this."

CHAPTER TWENTY-EIGHT
THE BEST THINGS IN LIFE ARE...

West doesn't hesitate. As soon as I point at the third passage, he grins and crawls through. Hannah is right on his heels. I follow them in, stopping in the dark tunnel when I hear something...

A siren.

Hannah and West have stopped too. Without their sneakers squeaking against the floors as they crawl, the only sound is the distant eerie wail.

It could be a car accident. Or maybe someone stumbled over a curb and fell down. Or maybe it's just a drill, and there's nothing bad happening outside at all.

Or it could be...

"You guys hear that?" West asks nervously. "You don't think that has anything to do with us, do you?"

More sirens blare. They sound like they're getting closer. A pit forms in my stomach.

"I'm sure it's nothing," I answer, nudging Hannah forward. West starts moving again too, pausing momentarily when he approaches the end of the tunnel. He helps Hannah out and onto her feet, then me. We're standing in another large mirrored room. The walls don't reach all the way to the ceiling again. This time I notice that the oddly shaped windows are on the opposite side of the room than they were when we came into this room. We must've gone in a circle.

Suddenly, the sirens outside stop. I let out the breath I've been holding.

I knew it was nothing. Nothing that involves us anyway.

"Hannah, West, and Sarah... This is the Maplewood Police Department!"

West's eyes grow so large they look like they could pop out of his head. Hannah's mouth has fallen open in a horrified *O* shape. She looks like a character straight out of a scary movie. Meanwhile, I'm imagining what handcuffs will feel like on my wrists.

"We know you're in there, and we want to see you get out safely." The booming voice continues.

West rakes a hand through his hair. "We're officially fugitives."

"We're not fugitives!" Hannah hisses. "Besides, they don't even sound angry."

I bite down on the inside of my cheek to keep from saying what's in my head, that even though they don't sound angry, they are. We lied. We snuck away. We broke into a funhouse. We worried everyone, and so far, I don't have anything to show for it.

"What do you guys want to do?" I ask. My voice breaks. My heart too.

I know what we decided earlier—that we'd keep trying until the bitter end, but I also know I love West and Hannah. I don't want to get them in any more trouble than they're already in. I've heard handcuffs are really uncomfortable. I imagine jail cells aren't much better.

West tilts his head to the side. "What do you mean?"

"I mean that we can ignore them and pretend like we aren't in here, *or* we can yell back to them right now. They might go easier on us if we...you know...cooperate."

Hannah runs her tongue over her front teeth. She looks unhappy, like she just swallowed a bug. "I don't want to cooperate. I want to find the treasure."

"Same," West says without hesitating.

"You guys don't have to do this." I tell them.

Hannah gives a half smile. The tip of her nose is still

darker than the rest of her face, and her normally shiny hair is flecked with bits of dust and cobweb. "We know that. We also know you'd do it for us."

I smile back. I would definitely do this for them. Hannah and West are the most perfect best friends a girl could ask for. Fierce, competitive, strong, and more than all that—thoughtful.

"Hannah, West, and Sarah...if you can hear us, stay where you are. I repeat, stay where you are. Do. Not. Move."

I didn't think it was possible, but the man yelling into the megaphone just got louder. And more serious.

"Don't move, huh?" Hannah asks, doing a silly little shimmy. "Whatever. Let's go, Deltas."

West gives me a quick reassuring squeeze and drops his backpack to the ground. I start scanning the new room. This one is filled with actual funhouse mirrors that distort everything. I wave my hand in front of the closest wall, where the mirrors make me look so thin that I'm like a spaghetti noodle. The wall on the opposite side where West is pacing makes him look as round as a beach ball. And Hannah is so short in some of the mirrors that she could be two instead of twelve. If I wasn't so nervous, this would be a fun place to take some pictures.

"This room is cool and all, but I don't see an exit. Do you guys?" West asks.

"Not yet, but there has to be one somewhere. Even if the triplets planned for this to be the final room, people who made it this far would need a way to get out." Hannah says, dipping into a plié as she stares at her squat reflection.

Somewhere deep in the walls, there's a thump. Then another.

I put my hand on the closest mirror, feeling for vibrations. There aren't any, but the thumping continues. When it stops, my blood runs cold.

"Oh no. They're coming in," I whisper. "The police are coming in!"

"All the more reason to find the exit!" West hisses. "I know I don't need to tell you guys this, but I'm going to anyway. If they catch up with us before we get to the actual end of this thing, it's bye-bye treasure."

"We'll never know if it's real or not," I say, the idea making me feel nauseous.

"Relax. It was hard for *us* to get this far. They'll never catch up." Hannah says, continuing her ballet. "William Taters couldn't get in, and that Conley guy was stuck in the first room."

"True. I doubt they have a lot of officers who are good at escape rooms." West puts his hand on the wall next to mine, feeling for any more evidence that they could be in the house. "But that doesn't mean they don't have saws and stuff to cut their way through."

Cut their way through? The idea is horrible. Not just because it means the police might actually reach us, but because it means they'd ruin what the triplets created. Now that we've come this far, I understand why Art Conley wanted to film his television show in here. There is something special about the funhouse, something magical. Yeah, it's covered in years of dust, and things aren't exactly the way they would have been if the triplets finished it, but it's still amazing. I don't want them to tear it apart.

Lost in her own world, Hannah does one more deep plié, then freezes down by the ground. She's in such an awkward frog-like squat that I almost laugh. "Guys. Guys! There's writing down here!"

West and I rush to her side. Sure enough, there are letters on the mirror. Words. Everything is backward, though.

"*This...how...house,*" I stutter, trying to read right to left instead of left to right. "It's so hard to read this way."

"Wait, I have an idea!" Hannah drops her bag and digs through it, then triumphantly holds up a compact. Turning so her back is to the mirror, she opens the compact and holds it up over her shoulder. "*This house you're in is nearly done. Just one more room, and then you've won. The door you seek requires no key. Like the best things in life, this one is...*"

She stops talking, looking stumped.

"Is what?" I ask, trying to look at the mirror over her shoulder.

Hannah squints. "I can't read that last word. Can someone wipe off that part of the mirror? It's blurry."

West drops down and uses his sleeve to rub at the glass. "The mirror is uneven here. Warped or something. Is this any better?"

"No," Hannah snaps. "Spit on it. It's still too blurry."

Annoyed, West blows a deep breath on the mirror then rubs at it, harder this time. Small flecks of something shiny begin flaking off and falling to the floor. West looks up, his eyes lit with amusement. "I was going to recommend glasses for you, Banana, but guess you don't need them after all. The triplets made this hard to read on purpose!"

When he's finally scraped off all the film covering the mirror, the real glass is visible. The word *free* is written backward in red ink. Also, the rectangular piece of mirror the word is written on isn't warped like West originally thought, but slightly raised, like a button.

Hannah reads the passage again, this time with the missing word in it. "*This house you're in is nearly done. Just one more room, and then you've won. The door you seek requires no key. Like the best things in life, this one is...free.*"

West looks from the word to me, then to Hannah. "This sounds good, right? Like I should push the button?"

It sounds like for once, trusting luck didn't backfire. When I chose door number three, I told myself no matter what happened, we'd be okay. *I'd* be okay. I'm not sure I actually believed that until just now.

Another thump echoes through the house.

"Yes!" I breathe out. "Push it! Do it now!"

West slaps his palm down on the mirror. And just like that, the entire panel of glass slides to the side.

CHAPTER TWENTY-NINE
DELTAS FOREVER

I rush through the new opening in the wall, excitement pulsing through me.

Just one more room, and then you've won. That's what the clue said, which means we did it. Right? This is the final room. It has to be.

West flips on the lantern, lighting up the space just enough for us to see the walls are painted in waves of color—reds, blues, greens, and bright purple splashed from the ceiling to the floor. My excitement fizzles out though when I realize that although the room is colorful, it's basically empty.

There's no treasure chest filled to the brim with gold.

No money fluttering from the ceiling, or even plain old

dollar bills stacked in piles. There's not even a banner or a sign that says we won.

It's so disappointing that tears spring to my eyes. Not small tears either, but the waterfall kind that sting the rims of your eyes and make you feel like an epic baby.

"I can't believe this," I say, my heart aching. "The treasure...there's no treasure."

There's no treasure because either it never existed, or the triplets stopped working on this house before they could get to it. The knowledge is so painful I can't hold in my sadness anymore. The tears break free, paving little paths through the dust and dirt I'm covered in.

"It's okay, Sarah," Hannah says, patting me gently on the back.

"I thought for sure there would be something. I really did." I sniffle into my sleeve, no longer caring if I walk out of here covered in snot. I'm going to end up moving to Michigan now anyway. "Guess the triplets made it all up."

I knew the probability of there being a treasure in this house wasn't good. But what I didn't know was how horrible I'd feel when I found out it didn't exist for sure. It's like realizing that magic and spells and unicorns aren't real. The world is just a little darker once you know it.

And this? Not finding a treasure is *nothing* like failing an escape room. It's so much worse. This time I failed at saving my house...my family.

Another siren echoes in from outside. More police. Or worse, firefighters with tools they'll use to destroy everything the triplets created. I'm angry with them, hurt even, but I still don't want to see their dream ruined. No one deserves that.

I spin in a panicked circle, noticing a circular opening in the wall on the opposite side of the room. There's a pole installed above it, kind of like the type of handle that you'd hold on to if you were going down a waterslide or a slide at the park.

A slide.

I remember seeing one on the side of the building. It was curvy and went all the way down to the ground. That has to be it! Of course, when I saw the slide the first time, I thought I'd be whooshing down it victoriously with a treasure in my lap.

Shaking off my sadness, I point to the door. "Here's the plan. The police are here. If we get caught in here, we're in trouble. Right now, they can't prove we were ever here."

"But we made a mess of all the rooms," Hannah says. "We broke stuff too."

"True, but they can't prove that was us. It could have been anyone." I wave my hands up toward the ceiling. "No cameras anywhere. We're safe. *If* we get out of here before the police catch up with us."

West's eyebrows jump. "What are you suggesting?"

"I think that is the slide that will get us back outside. If we go now, we might be able to get away from here without them ever seeing us," I say.

"What if the house is surrounded?" Hannah asks.

"It might be," I admit. "But they also might be trying to get through the house right now, which would mean they're all in here. This... I think this is our best shot."

I stick my fist out. West and Hannah do the same, bumping their knuckles into mine one final time. Even though my friends are smiling, their expressions are sad. They know how much I've just lost, how much *we* just lost. I'll probably be on a train to Michigan by morning.

Racing to the circular opening, I skid to a stop and wave West and Hannah over.

"You guys first. If anyone deserves to get out of this mess without a juvenile record, it's you."

For once, Hannah doesn't debate. She grabs the handle at the top, then turns to look at West and me. "Deltas forever," she says, tossing up the triangle symbol with her fingers before vanishing down into the darkness. West climbs in after her.

"I'll be right behind you," I say, putting a hand on his back to give him a shove.

He plants his feet against the sides so he doesn't slide. "I'm not sorry we did it."

I laugh weakly. "Well, you might be in a minute."

"No," he says, shaking his head. "I mean it. I'm glad we did this, and even if we get caught, I'm not sorry at all."

The pain in my heart dissolves just a little as I watch the edges of West's mouth quirk up into a half smile just before he disappears into the tunnel. It's so unlike West *not* to be upset about us being in trouble. That means even though we didn't find the treasure, today meant a lot to him too.

The slide is too long for me to hear exactly when West gets to the bottom, so I have to guess. Hopping up into the opening, I use the handle to lower myself down. Then I stop.

There's something odd about the top of the slide. Not just odd...familiar. The same equilateral triangular pattern we saw in the mirror maze is carved into the metal. I narrow my eyes in the darkness, noticing that one of the triangles looks different from the rest. Its edges are wider, more like gaps.

Excited, I push on the triangle but nothing happens. No biggie. Sometimes it takes several tries to uncover the clue we're digging for. And this looks like it could be a clue.

Tracing the outline of the triangle, my fingers stumble

over something protruding from the metal. I pull it and groan when it refuses to budge. It's not a handle. Maybe it's a latch? Using my feet to anchor myself in the mouth of the slide so I don't go down before I'm ready, I slide the tiny bolt to the side and gasp as the triangle door pops open and a folded yellow slip of paper falls out into my lap. It looks almost exactly like the one I came home and found pinned to the door of my house when the bank decided to take it back.

My stomach lurches with the memory. The foreclosure notice was the worst thing that has ever happened to me. Besides Dad getting sick, that is. Mom tried so hard to hide her crying that night, but I knew she was scared. I was too. Even Sean lost his appetite, and he normally eats like a rhino.

I'm dying to read the paper, but there isn't time. Instead, I shove it into my pocket and hold my breath.

There is one direction forward, one way you must go. Through locked rooms is a victory and something you know.

All this time I've been afraid. Afraid of letting my family down. Afraid of letting West and Hannah down. Afraid of ending up like William Taters, handcuffed and headed to jail for breaking into the funhouse. But my biggest fear—the fear that the treasure doesn't exist—already came true, and I survived it. I guess even though there's no treasure, the triplets' riddle was right about one thing. Getting to this room was a victory, and all their maddening tunnels, passages, and riddles did lead to something I know.

I know I can absolutely, 100 percent survive whatever is waiting for me at the bottom of this slide.

CHAPTER THIRTY
FATE SUCKS

I clamber into the slide, my heart splintered into a billion pieces. It hurts so much that I'm afraid it won't ever go back together. And even though this has been a huge disappointment, there's still a little piece of me that's hoping for something. An explanation at least. The end of most escape rooms is the best part. Sometimes there is victory music, sometimes confetti. Usually, the host rushes in and congratulates you. This room was bare and sad.

Why? Why would the triplets do something so mean? My thoughts land back on the paper in my pocket, the tiniest sliver of hope needling me.

Taking a deep breath, I press myself forward and let gravity take me. The slide is faster than I expect, curving and twisting in a way that would be so, *so* fun if things were different. If I had a treasure in my lap.

I hit the bottom, then shield my eyes, taking my first steps out into the sun. I don't make it very far before I feel arms around me.

"Sarah!" Mom grips me tighter than she ever has before. "What were you thinking? You could've been killed in there!"

I pull back and look into her tired, bloodshot eyes. "I'm sorry."

Her head dips. Pinching the bridge of her nose, she takes in a few deep breaths before looking at me again. "I was so scared. You really scared all of us."

Guilt floods me. "I didn't mean to. I just wanted to..." I pause and look up, realizing that West and Hannah didn't make it far. They're about twenty feet away, standing with their parents. Their *very* disappointed-looking parents. "I wanted to make things better for us. I thought if I could find the treasure, I could save our house. You know, fix things."

I shift from foot to foot, the mystery paper in my pocket practically whispering my name. I consider sneaking a peek at it, but Mom is staring at me, and the officers now standing by West and Hannah are furiously scribbling in tiny notebooks. Bad things, from the looks on their faces.

That's when I notice them. The police. They're

everywhere. Some are standing around by the front door of the house, some are sprinkled out in the tall grass, and at least a half dozen are investigating the bushes that cover the secret entrance we used. There are some news trucks on the road now as well. Probably here to film us getting arrested like they did Art Conley.

"Please don't let my friends get into trouble for this," I beg. "It was my idea. All this was me. They only came along because they wanted to help."

Sympathy flashes in my mother's expression. "I believe that, honey. I do. And I love you so, so much for caring and trying. But this was bad judgment on all your parts, and I can't guarantee they won't get into trouble. What you did today was a terrible idea ,and even though it was for"—she pauses with a gentle smile—"for noble reasons, you shouldn't have done it."

"Am we going to go to jail?" I ask.

She wraps her arm around me and tugs me to her side. "I don't think jail is in your future, kiddo, but you're definitely grounded, so I wouldn't celebrate just yet."

West and Hannah make their way over to us. They both have the same downtrodden expressions and hunched shoulders. Apparently, they got the *you're grounded for life* talk just now too.

"I'm going to go speak with the officers. You can have a

minute to say goodbye, and then we're going home, all right?" Mom asks. She brushes a stray cobweb off Hannah and reaches up to tousle West's hair, then realizes he's too tall and laughs.

"Thank you," I say, meaning it more than I ever have. Mom could be a real jerk about this if she wanted to be. And she'd have every right. Instead, she's being how she always is—understanding.

"I'm so sorry, guys." I say.

"Stop," West says. "We're fine. My dad just talked to the police officers, and it sounds like we aren't going to be in that much trouble."

I perk up. "But we broke in."

"Not really. I told them about the secret door in the side of the building. We didn't break any windows or locks to get in." He kicks at a rock in the grass. "Don't know if it will matter, but I tried."

"And I told them about the treasure and how the triplets basically invited people to look for it," Hannah adds.

I snort. "Yeah. Like seventy years ago."

"Still!" She exclaims. "We aren't the first people to do this. The police have bigger fish to fry."

Sneaking a glance around, I notice that no one is looking in my direction. I wiggle my fingers into my pocket and touch the paper. Hope pulses through me.

"Guys," I hiss, careful to keep my voice low. "Huddle up. I found something in there right before the police walked me out. It's probably nothing." I stop talking, then restart. "I'm sure it's nothing. But I grabbed it anyway."

West and Hannah crowd closer.

I fish the paper out, wincing at how crumpled it is. Even if it isn't the explanation I want from the triplets, it's the only memento I have from today. Well, other than some scrapes and a layer of dirt on my skin. I slowly unfold it, preparing myself to be disappointed again. It's probably a receipt for horse food or chickens or whatever people would have been buying in the 1950s.

Instead, there are big black letters in bold on the top.

CONGRATULATIONS!

CHAPTER THIRTY-ONE
CHARLIE BUCKET

I look up and West and Hannah, my heart racing.

"What does it say?" West asks.

The paper shakes in my hand. I glance back down at it and begin reading. "*Our game was cut short, but yours clearly was not. With challenges and riddles, this house has been fraught. You showed your true skills, and you took the lead. Your reward, our friend, is this...the deed.*"

"Deed?" Hannah repeats.

The riddle continues just below so I inhale a shaky breath and keep reading. "*Dream number one was to open, but alas that dream left. Dream number two was for someone to experience it yet. So please take our funhouse and do what you will. Open or sell, our wish is fulfilled.*"

Shifting the paper, I notice it's not actually just one, but two stuck together. The second sheet looks like a certificate. There's a smaller envelope taped to the back. I tear it open, gasping when a key falls out. It's a little larger than a normal key and has a triangular top. I turn it over in my hand, goose bumps rising all over me as I stare at the triangle—our symbol.

"Dream number one was to open, but alas that dream left," West repeats, this time saying each word slowly and carefully. "This riddle is about how the triplets didn't get the chance to open the funhouse, right?"

"I think so," I answer. "And the 'dream number two' part must just mean that even though they never opened it, they still wanted someone to enjoy it."

Someone like us. Three goofballs who love riddles, codes, and math. The same twinge of sadness hits me—the one I felt when I saw the pictures of this house for the first time. The triplets cared so much about their dream that they didn't let it go, even after one of them died. I guess they wanted this moment just as much as we did.

Hannah's mouth is hanging open. Her eyes dart from the paper to me. "So then the last part of that riddle means..."

Please take our funhouse and do what you will. Open or sell, our wish is fulfilled.

The words roll through my head like waves.

"Did we actually find the treasure?" I ask, holding the second sheet out to West and Hannah to examine. "Is it"—I wave my hand out at the funhouse—"this?"

West looks from the paper to me, then back to the paper again. "Holy crap. Holy crap. Ho—"

Hannah slaps a hand over his mouth. Her cheeks are flushed with color. "The Triplet Treasure. It *was* real." She throws her arms around me. "Sarah! You own a funhouse!"

I own a funhouse. Is that even possible?

"This is so Willy Wonka," West says breathlessly.

"What?" Hannah asks with a loud laugh.

West grins. "You know, Willy Wonka! He left his whole chocolate factory to a deserving kid. A kid who needed money for his family."

That would make me Charlie Bucket. I glance over at my mother, who is probably trying to convince the police that I'm not a criminal and they shouldn't haul me away to the nearest empty cell. The exhaustion of the past few years is written in the lines of her face, the boniness of her shoulders, and thinning arms. Working two jobs, sleeping too little, eating in the car and on breaks in between shifts—it's not healthy.

A chilly breeze picks up, fluttering the papers in my hands. I hang onto them tightly, reminded of an old movie Dad and I watched together. *The Goonies.* The kids were trying to save their neighborhood home by finding a pirate treasure. In the end, they thought they failed but they didn't thanks to a pocketful of jewels.

Maybe the deed is my jewels.

"Is this real? Am I hallucinating?" I ask, tears building again. Only this time they aren't tears of loss or sadness. They're tears of hope.

West and Hannah fold themselves around me. They smell terrible, like a gym uniform that hasn't been washed in months, but I don't care. They also smell like home, and maybe, just maybe, the triplets just gave me the chance to keep mine.

"It's real. This place is famous, Sarah. Even if your parents don't want to open the funhouse again, you can sell it," West says. "No Michigan for you!"

No Michigan. The thought is so incredible I almost burst into tears.

"Mom?" I yell.

She turns to face me.

I hold the papers up in the air, my smile so wide it hurts. "We beat the buzzer."

Those four words might not mean much to most people, but to the Deltas, they mean everything. I clench the papers tight in my hands, a future taking shape in my mind.

A bright, escape room–filled future.

EPILOGUE
SIX MONTHS LATER

October has always been one of my favorite months.

For one, Halloween decorations are amazing. Houses decked out in ghosts, goblins, witches, and spiderwebs make even the most boring neighborhoods fun. Same with little fake graveyards. It's all just a mood, and one I'm here for.

Halloween is also the only time of year you can be anyone you want to be and absolutely nobody can judge you. Like the time every girl in my second-grade class dressed as one princess or another, and I showed up in tattered clothes and zombie makeup. Had I been into odds back then, I would've known the chances of my costume fitting in were bad. But I wasn't and I didn't, and because Halloween is awesome, no one cared.

This Halloween, though, is hands down the best I've ever

had. For the first time in a while, I don't want to be anyone other than Sarah Greene.

"Are we ready?" Mom chirps, making eye contact with me in her rearview mirror. The bags and dark circles under her eyes aren't totally gone, but they're better. She's gained some weight too. Enough to make her look like Mom again.

"Ready," I say with a deep, calming breath. This day has been written in our calendar for months. My nerves jangle with excitement. News crews already line the streets, and dozens of neighbors are lined up, waiting for the big moment.

Hopping out of the car, I immediately move to open the front passenger door. It flies wide before I can get there.

"I can do it, kiddo," Dad says, beaming. He swings one foot out, then another before gripping the sides of the door and slowly rising.

It's something I wasn't sure I'd ever see again. Dad out of bed. Dad standing. Dad enjoying the sun, the breeze, the leaves. *Life.*

Remission from chronic fatigue syndrome happens, but I guess I never expected it to happen for Dad. It seemed like that dark room, that bed, and that stupid red applause button was his future. But everything changed when we discovered that the triangular key opened yet *another* hidden door to the funhouse. Inside, there was an office. Like everything else, it was covered in dust, but it was clear that was where the triplets planned to work once the house was open. And inside that office was one of the biggest surprises of all. A lockbox. Just as Karl and Hans left their marks on this funhouse with the epic library and detailed cabinetry, Stefan the banker left his mark with a small, metal box. Inside there were details on something called a trust and one final message.

AUDENTIS FORTUNA IUVAT.

Fortune favors the bold. It was the first message we saw when we entered the funhouse, and once I discovered that the triplets had left me with the deed to their funhouse, I understood how true it is. Because of that one day my life— no, *our* lives—changed.

Dad got more help.

Mom got our house back.

Sean got to go to his dream college.

And me? Well, I got to stay with West and Hannah.

Dad holds the cane he uses for balance in one hand and crooks the other arm out for me to take. It's like a fantasy, really. Being here again, back where it all started. Back where the triplets launched their biggest and boldest dream, and gave me back mine.

"It's beautiful, Sarah," Dad whispers as I lock my arm with his.

"It sure is," Mom adds, joining us.

My eyes glide across the lawn that was once ratty and overgrown to the funhouse. It looks so much different than the day West, Hannah, and I snuck in. The paint is brighter. The windows are open and sparkling, like eyes that just saw the line of people waiting to get in. Even the slide looks better—longer and windier, just like the triplets would have wanted. I was afraid I'd feel sad when we sold the funhouse, but I don't. This feels good. Right.

"We're going to head up to the house, sweetie," Dad unclasps his arm from mine and pulls me into a tight hug. "You'll meet us? It's supposed to start in about five minutes, I believe."

"Yup. I'll be right there."

Right after I finish breathing and reminding myself that nothing can take this day away from me, that is.

"Hey," West says, jogging up. He's smiling so big it warms me from the inside out. "Nice shirt."

I bump into him, laughing. We're wearing the same hoodie—a tie-dyed sweatshirt with a triangle on the front. Below, the text reads:

WELCOME TO THE DELTA GAME
FORTUNE FAVORS THE BOLD

"I still can't believe the new owner made these," I say, unzipping my jacket enough for my shirt to be visible.

"I can't believe who the new owner is," West says with a smirk.

I'm about to comment on that when a shriek rings out. Hannah is running across the lawn, her newly cropped blond hair flapping like wings at the side of her head.

She pulls up to the side of us, breathless and pink-cheeked. "Sorry, guys. I left my gum in the car and had to go back."

"Of course, you did," I say, laughing. "No amount of fame is gonna change your taste buds."

Winking, she snaps a loud bubble. "Totally. Forget caviar, no matter how popular the Delta Game gets, I'm spearmint for life."

West cracks up. The sound is a perfect soundtrack for the day.

Once the news broke about the Triplet Treasure being real, West, Hannah, and I ended up on the news. Different newspapers and television channels wanted to interview us nonstop. We were even on a podcast about abandoned buildings and something called urban exploring, which I now know just means breaking in (something I've learned you should never, ever do). Of course, it wasn't *all* good. West, Hannah, and

I got grounded. For three weeks! Funny thing is, I wasn't even grounded for sneaking into the funhouse. I was grounded for lying about it. When I think about how scared Mom must've been though, I understand. Things turned out okay, but we were lucky.

I twist the wishbone charm dangling from my necklace and smile. Luck wasn't something I ever believed in before— before the yellow slip of paper, the funhouse, and the treasure. Now I get it. Life throws curveballs sometimes. We can't always plan, can't always predict. But maybe, just maybe, with hard work and a little luck, we'll be okay.

No, not maybe. *Definitely*. I'm going to be okay.

"My parents are already up by the stage. You guys wanna go?" I ask.

Hannah and West nod, following me toward the house. Crowds have gathered, and a few news crews turn their cameras on us when they see us approach. The Deltas. I smile and wave to them, and Hannah spins a circle. West stops and throws his arms up in what I think is some bizarre superhero-like pose.

When we reach the front row where our parents are already seated, I take a moment to soak it all in. The energy. The excitement. The opening day of a funhouse that should've been selling tickets many, many years ago.

I wish you could see this, triplets. I wish you could see your dream coming true.

"Sixteen rooms," West says. It's about the billionth time he's said this, but it's fine with me. Most of the escape rooms we do are three or four spaces, and even though we didn't have to conquer all sixteen rooms in the triplets' funhouse, it's still the biggest and wildest one we've ever tried. And beat!

The front door of the funhouse creaks open. I hold my breath as a man walks out. Like the first time I met him, he's wearing a suit. But today his scruffy beard is cleaned up, and his blue eyes are brighter, like the sky after a storm.

William Taters.

William isn't the weirdo burglar everyone presumed him to be. He's just a dude who wanted to know more about his family history, and like us, made some sketchy decisions trying to find it. Looking at him now, I realize he's a lot like the funhouse; nothing is as it appears.

William hobbles to the center of the stage, then just like Willy Wonka himself, does a somersault and jumps back up with a flourish. The crowd goes wild.

"Welcome one, welcome all to the Delta Game!" he shouts into the microphone.

Applause echoes through the neighborhood.

"I cannot express how excited I am to be here today. Only a year ago, this building, the dream of my great grandfather Stefan, was a mystery to me. It was a piece of my family history I had no access to. Until these three." He walks to the edge of the stage and points at Hannah, West, and me.

Heat floods my cheeks. I should be used to the attention by now, but I'm not.

"These three tenacious young people managed to do what no one else, including myself"—he makes a sheepish face, and the audience laughs—"had ever done. They solved my great grandfather's riddles. They beat his codes. They found the hidden treasure." He pauses, tearing up. "And thanks to their kindness, I'm now the proud owner of the Delta Game—a funhouse that promises to be the best, longest, and most spectacular funhouse to ever exist!"

More clapping. This time, people begin standing. William swipes at his eyes, clearly emotional. I look over at my parents, a warm feeling rushing through me when I see they're smiling and holding hands.

"So let me be the first to welcome you all. In honor of my great grandfather Stefan Stein's dream, today's entry is free for all. Let's have some fun!" William takes a bow, and the whole neighborhood seems to erupt. Children are rushing toward the door, their parents hot on their heels.

I stand up and let my head tip back, so the sun hits my face. Even with the brisk Halloween-y air, it feels warm. Perfect. Like today.

We didn't just beat sixteen rooms in the funhouse, I realize as the crowd jostles excitedly around me. We beat our own fears. Luckily, William Taters is a pretty cool guy, and once the funhouse had been fixed up and was safe, he took us on a private tour of all the rooms we didn't discover our first time through. There was a room themed like an underwater treasure hunt, and one that felt like you were on a pirate ship. There was even one that involved plugging a bunch of codes into something called a switchboard. Every room was wilder than the last, and I still can't believe how creative the triplets were. I wish we could've met them.

"You kids heading in?" Mom asks. She helps Dad to a standing position, then slings her purse over her shoulder. "Pretty sure I recall Mr. Taters..." She pauses while West and Hannah giggle. They still haven't gotten over that name. "Pretty sure I recall that he invited you to be his special guests in there today."

He did. And we would, except that would goof up our other plans.

Looking back at the house, I shake my head. "We're taking a rain check."

Dad raises an eyebrow. "Wow. Turning down an escape room? Who are you and what have you done with my daughter?"

Laughing, I give him a hug. "Don't worry, she's still here. In fact, if she doesn't get on a train with these two goofballs soon, she'll miss her ticketed entry to *Vipers and Villains*."

"The newest," Hannah starts.

"And most challenging escape room offered at Escape City!" West finishes. They sound just like the commercial.

"No one has beaten the buzzer yet," I tell my parents with a sly smile. "Those are some crummy odds."

Dad chuckles. "Then why are you smiling?"

"Because there's a first time for everything."

ACKNOWLEDGMENTS

This book would not have been possible without the support of many, many people. Thank you to my agent Shannon Hassan and my editor, Annie Berger, for listening to this wacky idea and wholeheartedly backing it. To the team at Sourcebooks, thank you for letting me stretch my wings and try something new...something that was as exciting to me as the Triplet Treasure was to the Deltas.

To my husband, John, and my kids, Rob, Ben, and Ella —your constant enthusiasm and positivity means the world to me. I admire you all more than anyone in the world and having you along on this adventure with me means everything. I love you all so, so much.

To Jenni Walsh—this book would not have been

possible without your sharp eyes and brilliant feedback. Thank you!

And to my readers: thank you. Thank you for making the leap with me to a book that trades ghosts and graveyards for secret passages and trapdoors. I love this story and these characters and I hope you do, too.

Long live the Deltas!

ABOUT THE AUTHOR

Lindsay Currie is the author of six middle grade novels. She grew up on Nancy Drew and loves a good mystery. Bonus points if it's spooky! When she's not writing, Lindsay can generally be found looking for an adventure of her own. She loves researching the forgotten history in her city of Chicago, taking long walks with her family, and as pretty much everyone knows...Disney World! To find out more about Lindsay, please visit her website at www.lindsaycurrie.com.